Praise for Pamela Britton's
Playboy Prankster

"Playboy Prankster is hilarious ...entertaining story ...Really enjoyed the verbal banter"

~ *Sensual Reads*

"For the little boy inside the man that never quite grew up and all the women that love him. Playboy Prankster is good for a laugh and some truly great characters."

~ *Long and Short Reviews*

"Pamela Britton has written a fun, fast-paced story with two great characters."

~ *The Romance Studio*

Playboy Prankster

Pamela Britton

Samhain Publishing, Ltd.
577 Mulberry Street, Suite 1520
Macon, GA 31201
www.samhainpublishing.com

Playboy Prankster
Copyright © 2011 by Pamela Britton
Print ISBN: 978-1-60928-282-0
Digital ISBN: 978-1-60928-232-5

Editing by Tera Kleinfelter
Cover by Kanaxa

This book is a work of fiction. The names, characters, places, and incidents are products of the writer's imagination or have been used fictitiously and are not to be construed as real. Any resemblance to persons, living or dead, actual events, locale or organizations is entirely coincidental.

All Rights Are Reserved. No part of this book may be used or reproduced in any manner whatsoever without written permission, except in the case of brief quotations embodied in critical articles and reviews.

First Samhain Publishing, Ltd. electronic publication: October 2010
First Samhain Publishing, Ltd. print publication: September 2011

Dedication

This one's for my sisters. You're the best siblings a girl could ever have and I thank God for you guys every day. Thanks for being such great aunts to Codi. We love you.

Chapter One

He was Trouble. And Trouble was CJ's mantra.

Tan. Rich. Overconfident. Unsuitable. Bachelor. Lacking. Ethics.

T.R.O.U.B.L.E.

This particular Trouble, aka Bryce Danvers, leaned against the side of a big rig, the afternoon sun casting shadows on his angular face. Race trucks zoomed off into the desert. People milled around the staging area looking for their favorite movie star, professional driver or celebrity millionaire slated to drive in the Charity Pro/Am 2000. But Trouble seemed oblivious to it all because Trouble was talking to a cotton-candy blonde with a tight, pink, mini-skirt thingie vacuum packed to her body.

Figured.

"I just love your toy store commercials," the blonde gushed.

CJ checked her stride, hanging just a few feet away from them. This ought to be good.

"Do you? Which is your favorite?" Bryce Danvers asked.

Oh, pul-leez.

"The one where all the baby toys come alive."

Yeah, probably because she couldn't figure out her own Speak and Spell. CJ side-stepped an overzealous spectator.

"Oh yeah?" Bryce smiled down at the blonde with what

could only be called a predatory grin, his black hair rustling in the dusty breeze. "Do you want to get together tonight and talk about them?"

Talk? Yeah, right. As if the blonde woman had worn the dress as part of a shrink-wrap experiment.

"Sure, Bryce, I'd love to."

Get naked with him, she meant.

"Where're you staying?"

At a place which rents rooms by the hour, where else?

"The Star Motel."

Told you.

"When can I pick you up?"

Let's see. Give her two hours for the hair, an hour for the makeup, three hours for her to find her motel again…

"How about seven?"

"Sounds great."

She just bet it sounded great.

Okay, okay, so she was obviously in a rank mood, but she'd been that way ever since she'd been told by her editor she'd have to sit in the same race truck as Bryce Danvers. Still, that didn't excuse being such a cat. Jealousy, she admitted, eyeing the blonde. And who wouldn't be? The last time she'd looked good in anything that tight had been about sandbox age.

She wiped her palms against her jeans and shoved off to meet Mr. Trouble.

"Hi," she said brightly when Bryce managed to tear his blue eyes away from the blonde's breast implants.

"Hi, yourself." His Southern drawl washed over her like the chords of Clint Black's guitar.

"I'm CJ Randall."

"Hi, CJ Randall." His mouth curved into a flirtatious smile. Bryce Danvers with a flirtatious smile was a Bryce Danvers who should come with a warning sign. Caution—Respirator Required Beyond This Point.

Apparently, the woman in pink thought so too. Her voice sounded a bit breathless as she said, "Bryce, honey, perhaps we should talk somewhere else, away from all these...people." Her gaze slid contemptuously down to CJ's jeans and T-shirt, but CJ ignored her. She refused to be intimidated by a woman whose hair probably weighed more than her brain. Besides, it was obvious talking wasn't all the blonde wanted to do. Heck, no woman in her right mind would waste her time talking to Bryce Danvers. But that's *exactly* what CJ was here to do. Talk to him—for three days straight—while conducting her very first in-action interview from the passenger seat of his one-ton, twelve hundred horsepower Dodge Ram.

Oh, joy.

"Actually, I need to speak to you too," CJ said.

Bryce lifted a curious, adorable black brow and CJ's throat went dry. "I'm from *DRIVE Magazine*, and I'm your co-pilot for the race."

Silence greeted her words as someone jostled her from behind. Bryce stared down at her as if a big wad of dirt hung off the end of her nose.

"*You're* CJ Randall?" he repeated in disbelief.

CJ nodded, then swiped above her lip...just in case.

"But...you're not a man."

"Gee, really?" Gosh, she was sick of hearing that. People always assumed her initials stood for a guy's name.

"I meant, your editor told us he was sending a man." Bryce looked amused. Pink Pumps snorted. CJ stared up at Bryce in shock. It couldn't be.

But it was.

Miles Van Dyke, Editor-From-Hell, had set her up. Little worm. No wonder he'd had that nefarious grin on his face when she'd left the office yesterday. All during the flight from Los Angeles to Las Vegas she'd wondered about it.

"Is that a problem?" she asked. It came out sounding more like a challenge than a question.

"Not that I can see," he replied silkily. His eyes broke contact to examine her. "But it might be with the owner of this truck. After all, you're his liability if I kill you."

"Are you saying that as a woman I'm more of a liability than a man?"

"Just a helluva shame to endanger such a pretty neck."

Oh great. He was a playboy *and* a flirt. But as his words sank in she tried not to panic. She couldn't afford to lose this assignment, not with Miles Van Dyke breathing down her neck, and not when her finances had dropped lower than the Dow Jones average on Black Monday. After the fiasco of her last job, if she lost this one she could kiss her journalistic career goodbye. "If you're concerned about my qualifications, let me assure you I can handle the job."

Pink Pumps snorted again—or maybe she was letting air out from her swollen head. CJ wasn't sure.

"It's not up to me." Bryce shrugged.

"I know. But... Well..." Oh, darn. Why couldn't things be easy for once? "I'd like to discuss this with Mr. Santini." *Be firm, CJ.* The owner of the Star Oil race team had to let her go along.

"Sure." Bryce pushed himself away from the truck.

Some of the tension drained from CJ's shoulders, not much, but enough so she didn't feel like a linebacker for the

Rams.

"But, Bryce," Pink Pumps interjected. "What about *us*?"

Puuuleez. CJ wanted to shake her. Her whole future could be at stake and Hairspray Head was worried about playing hide the salami with Mr. Toy Store Mogul. Bryce must have read her mind because CJ could have sworn he shot CJ a look that said, "I'd go belly-to-belly with the little blonde in a minute."

He wrenched up his smile, then turned back to Pinkie. CJ almost felt sorry for the woman. No female under the age of ninety should have to endure such a grin.

"I'll catch up with you later," he said.

I bet, CJ thought wryly.

"You mean here?" Pinkie asked, shifting on her heels like a race horse waiting to ram the gate.

"Sure. I'll meet you back here in about an hour."

Jeeze, the broad was pushy, and the man was smooth, CJ'd give him that much. Of course, she'd known that about him. Bryce's reputation as a playboy was just about as famous as his toy store chain.

"Great!" The woman actually gushed.

She watched as Bryce smiled back. Pinkie tossed her empty little head, but not before she shot CJ a triumphant Cheshire grin lacking only the whiskers to make it complete. CJ wished her well in the chase of Bryce, though the woman might find that hard to believe. Personally, she had no intention of getting involved with a man who looked like Bryce, not after the last time she'd let passion rule her actions. She'd not only lost her job, she'd damaged her reputation. Now that she was finally back to work after two years of forced retirement she wasn't going to get involved with a man who'd do the horizontal mambo with Pinkie.

The crowd thinned as CJ and Bryce wound their way through the huge big rigs hauling the trucks around. Beyond the forty or so haulers was a parking lot. Desert cacti stuck up like sign posts between a mass of cars. To the right of the lot was a grove of campers.

They found Harry Santini, owner of the Star Oil race truck, in his RV. The monstrous thing looked more like Mick Jagger's touring bus than a recreational vehicle. He was lying face down on a plush orange sofa, his smoldering cigar filling the air with noxious waste. A lanky brunette looked up, then went back to massaging his back, her fingers delving beneath the neck of his white polo shirt. The woman had breasts the size of the Sierras, and lips so full she could have been in a movie titled Pump Friction or something. TV noise flickered in the background. Someone grunted. The roar of a crowd filled the room, followed by the nasal voice of a commentator. Tennis.

"What is it, Bryce?"

They both turned. Mr. Santini hadn't bothered to look up, Betty Boobs apparently doing too good a job to warrant movement. CJ studied what she could see of Bryce's long-time friend. He appeared heavier than in his pictures, but the gray hair was the same. With his head turned away she couldn't see his face, which was a pity. She'd like to look into the eyes of a man who'd gotten rich selling toys...the leather whip kind, that is.

"I want you to meet someone." Bryce bent down to shove three pillows off a small couch directly opposite Harry. He plopped himself down, somehow managing to look better against an orange backdrop. The window behind him threw soft light onto his face, making his five o'clock shadow even darker. Next, he released the Velcro strip holding his white and blue firesuit closed. CJ glanced down at him and had to force herself to look away from the thatch of dark, curling chest hair.

"Who?" Santini asked, startling CJ, who'd been wondering if race trucks had back seats.

"The journalist."

Mr. Santini still didn't look up, although the woman massaging him did. She glanced at CJ, wrinkled her nose, then honed in on Bryce with diamond-tipped precision. The smile she shot him was an open invitation lacking only her phone number. Yup, Bryce was a bimbo magnet. No doubt about it.

"Who?" Santini repeated, sounding impatient.

"CJ Randall," Bryce answered, clearly enjoying the moment. "The journalist from *DRIVE Magazine*."

Santini shifted. CJ mentally braced herself. Gray eyes met hers, white, bushy brows drawing up and up and up. "*That's* CJ Randall?" he all but shouted, pushing himself into a sitting position and nearly smacking his head into the brunette's. CJ winced. She'd been hoping for something a little more positive.

"In the flesh." Bryce leaned back, stretching out his long legs.

"How do you do, Mr. Santini?" Taking the bull by the horns, she went forward and offered her hand.

Santini just about swatted it away. "Silvia, why don't you leave us for a sec, hon?"

The brunette nodded, darting another glance at CJ. What she saw apparently impressed her about as much as dog doo. She sniffed as if she actually smelled it, then exited stage left. The door admitted a blast of desert heat behind her.

"Is this one of your pranks, Bryce?" Santini asked when they were alone.

"Nope."

"Mr. Santini," CJ interjected, tired of Bryce's amusement at her expense. "Perhaps I can explain. I'm new to *DRIVE*

Magazine and I'm sure my editor didn't think—"

"You're new?" the man squawked. "They sent someone to me who doesn't know squat about off-road racing?"

"Well, not exactly," CJ hedged.

"What do you mean not exactly?"

"I, well, I..." *Oh good, CJ. Great time to have a brain meltdown.*

"Do you or don't you?"

"Yes," she said firmly.

Santini looked far from convinced. He leaned back and crossed his arms in front of him, seeming not to notice the ashes that fell onto his tan slacks. "What's a chit?"

The question threw her. He was testing her, she realized. "Something a bird does on your shoulder?" she said, hoping to make him laugh.

Bryce chuckled. CJ had a hard time holding back a laugh too. Unfortunately, Mr. Santini didn't seem as amused. "Nice try," he snapped.

Party pooper. She'd have thought a man who made adult toys for a living would have a better sense of humor. Guess she could scratch charming him with her stunning wit.

"It's a marker," she said when it looked as if he was going to shove her out the door himself. "The officials give them to you along the course. At the end of the race, you have to have all your chits in order to prove you ran the course. If you don't, you're disqualified."

Santini looked startled, but then his bushy gray brows lowered. "Name the computer system we use to keep drivers on course."

CJ considered the question for a moment. "What is Global Positioning?"

"How does this race differ from other off-road races?"

That one she could answer too. "There's two divisions, one for professional drivers and one for non-professionals, like Bryce. It's run over a period of three days, twelve hours each stint, unlike traditional off-road racing, which is usually run over a period of twenty-four hours or less. At the end of the race, the driver with the best average time will win." There, that hadn't sounded too bad. "Oh, and real off-road trucks don't have front windshields," she added.

Santini looked about to sling another question at her but Bryce interrupted him. "Come on, Harry. It's not as if she's asking to drive."

Oh man. His voice shivered up and down her spine. *Stop it, spine. You are not getting involved with a millionaire playboy.* Especially when this one had a reputation to put a rock band to shame. Trouble.

"I don't like it. It's too dangerous for a woman."

CJ lost her patience. She wasn't trying to get into the NFL for criminey's sake. It was a stupid *race.* Drive from Point A to Point B. She didn't proclaim herself an expert on the subject, but she hardly thought it'd take more than a leathery behind to get her through the darn thing. Besides, she had an ace up her sleeve.

CJ smiled sweetly. "Mr. Santini, what do you think your sponsor, Star Oil, will say when they learn you turned down national exposure via a magazine article simply because the reporter was a woman?"

She had him. She knew it the moment she said it. Still, the silence stretched on as he struggled with his options. The TV had switched to auto racing. The drone of high horsepower engines faded in and out in the background. The pungent stench of cigar smoke drifted lazily through the air.

"Do you know what it's going to be like out there?" he asked at last.

CJ swallowed. "Well, not exactly, but I—"

"It's hell. Purgatory on wheels. You'll be lucky if you don't toss your cookies five minutes into the race. The heat sucks the life right out of you. There're no bathrooms, no air conditioning, nothing but you, the truck and Bryce. Hell, I'm not even sure Bryce is going to make it."

Blunt, yet effective.

"But I'll tell you what," Santini continued. "The first fueling stop is about an hour into the race. I'll let you ride with him for sixty minutes. And if you pass that test, an hour the next day, and then an hour the next. You can do your interviewing when we hit the hotels at night."

Well, it wasn't much, but it was better than nothing. "I appreciate that, Mr. Santini."

"Yeah, well, I doubt you'll thank me tomorrow."

She had a sinking suspicion that was true. Frankly, she'd done a little research into off road racing. What she had seen on-line had scared her to pieces. The realization that tomorrow she'd be a passenger in Bryce's vehicle caused her stomach to spasm in an all-too-familiar way. Her nerves had a way of dribbling out…one way or the other.

"Be here tomorrow morning at six forty-five."

She nodded, headed toward the door. Did they have public restrooms on-site?

Bryce shot up from the couch, opening it for her. "See you in the morning," he drawled softly.

CJ looked up, then wished she hadn't. He stared down at her lazily, his blue eyes making her wish she had cotton-candy hair and snow-cone boobs.

"Hey, you don't think it'll be that bad, do you?" And though she tried to keep her voice from cracking, it didn't work.

He smiled, a cocky boyish grin all the more adorable for the touch of compassion in his eyes. "It'll be okay, just relax."

"Relax," she repeated, nodding. Yeah, right.

Chapter Two

Relax, CJ reminded herself the next morning.

Yeah, right.

How was she supposed to relax when she was surrounded by the very trucks that gave her the heebie-jeebies? It was nearly seventy degrees out even though it was barely six. Already the asphalt radiated heat. They were on the edge of a town that boasted little more than a post office and a grocery store whose parking lot had been commandeered for the event. Obviously, the start of the Celebrity Pro/Am was the biggest thing to hit the area in a long time—at least judging by the amount of people milling about. It was still so early the sky resembled the color of dirty water. And yet she could barely move there were so many bodies scattered around the various big rigs and race trucks.

"Excuse me," she said, nearly clipping someone in the heels with her suitcase. She pushed it in front of her since she worried someone might trip over it if she drug it behind.

"No problem," a man said, barely sparing her a glance.

Story of her life.

"Mr. Danvers," she heard someone call, a child someone, CJ coming to a standstill. What was a kid doing here so early? Not even the birds were up yet.

"I can't believe it's really you. Did you bring us some toys?"

It didn't take her long to spot the child in question, especially since the little boy was surrounded by other kids his own age.

What was this?

"Toys?" Bryce said, the skin near the corner of his eyes crinkling his smile was so big. He wore a black firesuit, more than a few people hovering nearby when they recognized the celebrity children's toy store mogul whose commercial aired nationwide. More than a few scraps of paper were suddenly held out in his direction, Bryce scribbling his name without breaking eye-contact with the kids. "Now what makes you think I would have any toys?"

"Silly," a cute little blonde girl said. "You own a toy store."

Or two, or three, or four-hundred, CJ silently added.

The original little boy who'd spoken—he couldn't be any more than six or seven—bounced up and down on his toes. "And you told Mr. Jeffries you'd bring us some," he said with a grin. His two front teeth were missing.

CJ scooted closer.

"But I'm at a race," Bryce teased. "Why would I bring my toys *here*?"

This time a brown-haired girl stepped forward, one with frizzy hair and eyes nearly the same color as Bryce's. "Because you knew we were coming," she said, her face utterly serious.

The parent of the children smiled—or was it a parent? The more CJ studied the older woman, the more she recognized the lady might not be related to the kids surrounding her. She wore a dark business suit, CJ thinking the poor lady would be boiling in a couple of hours.

"You're right," Bryce said, his smile encompassing the

group. "I *did* know."

By now the crowd had thickened. As one of the celebrities this was part of the deal. While there were undoubtedly some serious off-road race fans milling about, most of the spectators had come out to see people like Bryce—famous people.

Bryce must have noticed the growing crowd too. He motioned the children's escort forward with a hand. "Come on," he said. "I might have something stashed away."

"Hooray," the boy cried as the crowd fell back.

CJ found herself following. At a distance, of course, but following nonetheless, her suitcase nearly clipping her heels. She sensed a story here somewhere. Too bad her camera had been packed away. She didn't relish the thought of opening her suitcase in front of everyone. With her luck all her underwear would spill out. But it sure would be nice to get a picture of Bryce with all the kids.

He led them to the transporter, a big rig that they used to haul the race cars around in, and that looked more like a rolling office than a mobile garage—at least judging by the pictures she'd seen amidst *DRIVE Magazine's* pages.

"Come on," she heard him say, pausing beneath an overhang. CJ hung back, her hand resting on the handle of her rolling overnight bag. She'd had to bring the darn thing along with her since she'd turned in her rental car this morning. Hopefully someone wouldn't mind bringing it to the next rest stop...and her, too. Otherwise she'd have to rent another car out in the middle of nowhere.

The pack of kids disappeared inside, the older woman turning to shut the sliding glass doors behind her.

And that was that.

But her curiosity had been aroused. She shoved off again, nearly clocking someone in the leg. "Sorry," she said. She stopped when she reached the side of the truck that she'd be riding in.

Riding in.

Her stomach curdled.

"What's going on?" she asked a mechanic who stood by the race truck, hoping to distract herself.

"What do you mean?" the burly man asked, his black shirt sporting the red star synonymous with their sponsor, Star Oil.

"All those kids following Mr. Danvers around."

"Oh, that," the man said, the wrench he held catching the sun and temporarily blinding CJ. "They're local foster kids."

"What are they doing here?" she asked.

The man shrugged. He had really wide shoulders, CJ wondering how he managed to cram himself inside the engine compartment when the need arose. "Don't know, but I heard talk that he's famous for doing stuff like this. Seems the man really likes kids."

Did he now, CJ mused, spotting her story's angle.

"By the way," he said, CJ noticing then that his name was Gus, at least if the stitching on his shirt pocket was to be believed. "We adjusted the seat belts for you. If you get in and they're too tight, just let us know. We can make them bigger."

And CJ's stomach flipped all over again. "Oh, ah, thanks."

"No problem," the man said with a wide smile. "Never had a woman ride in Betsy before." He tapped the side of the truck with his hand.

Betsy? The truck had a name?

"Had to change out the seat too."

"You can do that?" she asked.

"Yup. Bryce had one custom made for him. Cuts down on

your bouncing around."

That was good to know, especially if she ended up peeing her pants.

You're not going to pee your pants.

No, but she might vomit. Especially if her stomach didn't settle down. She'd taken some Dramamine earlier, but she suspected it wasn't going to help.

"Here we go."

CJ turned toward the transporter in time to see Bryce step out, his smile as wide as the double door he stepped between.

"Who wants to be the first person to sit inside?"

The little boy from earlier raised his hand. "Me, me!"

Blond, blue-eyed, and entirely too adorable, CJ wished she could bottle his enthusiasm. She was tempted to ask if he wanted to take her place today, then thought better of it. Bryce was approaching and she needed to project confidence and determination. "Good morning, Mr. Danvers," she said brightly when he noticed her standing there.

"CJ." His gaze rested on her suitcase. She saw his lips twitch. "You made it."

"I did." She could feel her lips tremble when she smiled. "I was hoping you could stash my suitcase someplace."

He looked down at the brown bag again. "Sure," he said, nodding at Gus who came forward and took the thing from her.

"Thanks," she said.

Where in the world did he get those blue eyes? His mom? Dad? When she'd done her research she'd heard no mention of his parents. In hindsight that seemed a little odd. Given his success it seemed she'd have run into some mention of them. "Of course." She mustered a smile for his tiny little posse, all of whom stared up at her in curiosity. "And who have we here?"

"These are some new friends," Bryce said. "Daniel, Marybeth, Samson, Patti and Laurie." He pointed them all out.

How he'd managed to remember all their names was anybody's guess, but CJ was impressed nonetheless. "Hey, guys." Her eyes caught on one of the little girls who held a new stuffed toy. They all held something in their hands: a new Lego set for one, another stuffed animal for the other little girl, a Barbie for one of the girls and a toy truck that bore a striking resemblance to the vehicle next to her.

"CJ here is going to ride along with me." Bryce said the words with a wide smile.

"You are?" the little boy who held the truck cried out. His name was Daniel. "You're soooo lucky."

"Am I?" Suddenly CJ's mouth was dry. Nerves, she told herself. She was *not* reacting to Bryce's presence.

"I would *kill* to ride in one of these things," the little boy added.

Not me. But she didn't say that.

"Come one," Bryce said. "You might not be able to ride in one, but you can sure sit inside."

CJ stepped back. Gus asked if anyone wanted to stand in the bed of the truck. One of the girls lifted a hand and CJ found herself tempted to dig through her underwear and find her camera. But her disappointment quickly faded away as she watched Bryce interact with his little guests. Gone was the playboy from yesterday, in his place stood a man who brought a soft smile to her face. Who made her think there was another side of him. A side that the public rarely saw. No wonder he owned a chain of children's toy stores. He clearly loved kids.

"Who wants a picture of themselves driving the truck?" Bryce called out.

Picture? CJ glanced around. The woman who'd accompanied the kids stepped forward, camera in hand. Ooo. Perfect. She'd ask her for copies later.

"I do," Daniel said.

The little brunette bumped into CJ's leg, the little girl glancing up at her in concern. "It's okay." CJ squatted down next to her.

"I don't want to get inside," the child admitted, her brown eyes wide. She had to be younger than Daniel by at least two years. Five she guessed.

"I don't either," CJ admitted, her gaze flitting over the truck. It was huge, various stickers and decals plastered across its white surface. She'd need a step ladder to get inside. The tires alone were almost as tall as the little girl standing next to her.

"You don't?" the girl asked.

CJ shook her head. "Nope. But I have to."

"Why?" the girl asked, pulling her Barbie box closer.

"Because I work for an evil ogre."

"You do?"

"I do. One who's mad at me for something I did and so he placed a curse on me. I have to ride in this truck for an hour. If I don't, he'll banish me from his kingdom."

"Oh," was all Marybeth said.

CJ found herself smiling, a pair of legs catching her attention. Bryce.

"An evil ogre," he said.

She slowly stood. "Yup," she said with a lift of her chin. "That's my boss."

"Then why don't you *let* him banish you from his

kingdom?"

He'd heard that? "It's not that simple," she found herself saying.

He looked so sincerely concerned for her welfare that CJ found herself thinking Pink Pumps had good taste.

Whoa, Ceej. You need to get a handle on those types of thoughts. Trouble, remember.

"Hmm," he mused. "Then I'm sorry to be the bearer of bad news." He turned to the group in question. "They're about to push the truck to the start/finish line."

Which meant it was time to take off.

"Aww, man," Daniel moaned.

"But we'll see you after," Bryce said brightly.

If she made it out alive.

He must have caught the look on her face because he patted her shoulder. "Hey. Don't panic. I promise to keep you safe."

"Yeah," she croaked. "Famous last words."

She looked terrified, Bryce observed less than a half-hour later. In fact, CJ looked about as comfortable as a patient in a dentist chair. He clutched his hands around the rubber coated steering wheel of the truck and darted another glance at the woman sitting alongside him. Yup. Green as the desert cacti dotting the landscape. And she just about flew out of her seat when Harry's voice boomed over the sound of the truck's revving motor, "Five minutes, Bryce. Have CJ put her helmet on."

Bryce peered through the black net which covered both driver and passenger windows and raised his hand to let Harry know he'd heard him. He glanced at CJ.

She'd drawn her shoulder-length brown hair into a ponytail, her profile clearly revealed. She had a cute nose. Kinda snub with little freckles dotting the tip. Pixie. He'd never used the word to describe a woman, but it fit CJ to a T. Like one of those women in a soap commercials. All clean and tidy. Smelled like it too. Mmm. Borax handscrub.

"Put your helmet on," he said when she didn't move.

She jerked around, then suddenly crammed her white helmet over her ponytail and head. Gone was the confident woman who'd spoken so softly to Marybeth. In her place sat a woman who was clearly on edge. He smiled reassuringly, but she didn't notice.

The truck in front of them scattered a plume of dust as it took off. Bryce watched as the cloud dissipated, revealing a green and yellow truck racing off into the desert. People dotted either side of the starting line, their heads cocked to follow the departing vehicles. Dust filled his mouth. He hoped to God when it was his turn to take off he didn't hit anybody. That would be a nightmare. For a moment or two he thought about asking Harry to tell the kids from Harmony Haven to back away.

Ridiculous, he told himself. He could *do* this. Piece of cake. And thankfully, once he cleared the staging area there'd be less chance to maim someone other than himself or his passenger. Speaking of whom...

He glanced at CJ again. Little spitfire appeared ready to throw herself out of the truck window. Either that, or have a nervous breakdown. Her green eyes were as wide as the R.P.M. dial. Her left hand fidgeted with the numerous belts strapping her in. She kept glancing at the Port-O-Potty off to her right, as if she contemplated making a run for it. He didn't blame her. Heck, he gave the woman credit for getting this far.

Harry had bet him last night she wouldn't show up. Harry had been wrong.

Not only had she shown up early enough that she'd been able to meet the kids from Harmony Haven, but she'd been toting a brown Samsonite suitcase like he was shuttling her to a desert spa. He supposed it a sign of her optimism that she thought she'd last the hour. He had to admire the woman for that. Actually, there were a lot of things about her that intrigued him. She'd looked so cute kneeling down beside Marybeth.

Odd, that. He hadn't taken note of a woman since he'd caught his ex-fiancée in bed with someone else—a female someone else. He frowned, not wanting to think about it. He'd rather think about CJ Randall.

She'd taken him by surprise from the first moment he'd seen her blush. He hadn't even known women could do that anymore. But she had, turning an impossible shade of red which made her cute little freckles stand out...and then later, she'd looked ready to vomit when Harry had done his best to discourage her from riding along, and still she'd stood her ground. This morning she'd been at ease around the kids he'd invited to the staging area. He liked women who didn't mind spending time with children.

"*Two minutes, Bryce.*"

Harry's voice crackled through the ear-pieces. Bryce wished he'd stop yelling. He was scaring the woman with his pre-shuttle countdown. She'd started to pant, and since the two helmets were connected on an open mic, her breaths echoed around them like Darth Vader's. Thank God Harry couldn't hear them unless Bryce pressed the mic button on his steering wheel. If he had any idea of how terrified his passenger was, he'd have pulled her from riding along.

She continued to fidget, only now her right hand joined the action, plucking at the white and blue lightweight firesuit she wore. She'd hyperventilate if he didn't do something soon.

"It'll be all right," he said softly, reaching out a hand to pat her leg.

She jumped.

He patted some more.

"*Sixty seconds, Bryce.*"

The look she turned on him was one he'd associate with a dog just before it was put to sleep.

"I'm terrified," she admitted.

Bryce reached out and stroked her thigh again, surprised at the little jolt of energy that shivered through his hand. Probably the static in the desert air. He certainly wasn't attracted to her. Oh, she was cute in a tomboyish sort of way. *Definitely* not his type, he reiterated. But tomboy or not, she needed to settle down before he had to call the paramedics.

"We'll be okay. If the truck tips over the most that will happen is we hang upside down for a few minutes."

Apparently, that wasn't the right thing to say.

"Oh, Gawd!" She started fumbling with her racing harness.

"*Ten seconds, Bryce.*"

"What are you doing?"

"*Nine.*"

"I'm getting out."

"*Eight.*"

"No you aren't. Just think how disappointed Marybeth will be."

"*Seven.*"

"She'll learn to live with her disappointment."

"*Six.*"

"Just sit back and enjoy the ride."

"*Five.*"

"Enjoy? Hah! Darn it, how do you get this seatbelt off?"

"*Four.*"

"Hold on, CJ. We'll be on our away in a sec."

"*Three.*"

"I don't want to be on our way, I want out."

"*Two.*"

"There's no time."

"*One.*"

"Too late."

"Oh, Gawd," CJ screamed again a heartbeat later. The starter waved his green flag. The idling motor roared to life. The lurch of the vehicle slung her back.

"Hold on," Bryce twanged in his Southern drawl.

Hold on? What was there to hold on to? The interior of the truck was bare sheet metal with three inch poles intersecting at odd angles—like some kind of sick jungle gym. Besides, she couldn't move if her life depended on it. The Gs were too strong.

And then she saw why Bryce'd told her to hold on.

The road disappeared.

"Hoooooly," she screeched just before they dropped off the edge of the planet. They were in the air forever. The 4x4 landed with a helmet-jarring thunk and the world went black. It took her a moment to determine it was the helmet. She pushed it back up, then immediately wished she hadn't. The world started to whiz by at a dizzying speed. Faster and faster they flew, desert scrub and rocks sliding past them.

"It's pretty smooth from here on out."

CJ clutched the seat. Why did she get the feeling Bryce's idea of smooth and hers were two different things? The truck bounced over the countryside like a boat skipping a wake; CJ's insides churned. She was going to have bruises tomorrow. Lots of them. *It's only for an hour, CJ. You can handle it.*

"If you want to look at the map it might help take your mind off it."

Mind? What mind? She'd lost hers the moment Bryce had hefted her into this one-ton nightmare. Lord, she could *still* feel where his hands had clasped her waist when he'd lifted her onto the sill of the truck.

Settle down, CJ. You'll be okay. Bryce knows what he's doing.

But he didn't *look* super confident. He stared straight ahead, his brow furrowed in concentration as he navigated the barely there dirt road before him. He must have sensed her stare for he flashed her a look. Even in that brief glance she saw the concern in his sky-blue eyes, so much of it that CJ's toes curled into a ball.

"I get car sick."

He cast her a startled glance. "You get *what?*"

"Car sick. Ever since I was a little girl. Reading in the car only makes it worse."

He looked at her as if she'd suddenly announced she was a resident of Mars. "You get car sick and you work for a car magazine?"

"It was supposed to be a desk job," she moaned, the motion upsetting her sensitive stomach even more. The truck skipped over the road like a pebble on a pond.

"So why'd you agree to do this?"

"Desperate," she groaned.

"For what? A barf bag?"

They careened over a particularly nasty bump. CJ clutched her belly and groaned. "Did you have to say tha...?" She reached up and tried to unclip the net thing covering the window.

"What're you doing?'

"Fresh air."

"You can't do that."

"Wh'not?"

"Because we're going too fast. If you stick your head out, the wind'll catch your helmet and rip your head off."

Oh, was that all? But there was a solution to her problem. She could just decapitate herself. But oddly, just tilting her head a bit seemed to help. Air gusted against her face. She closed her eyes. Bliss.

"Hold on."

Her lids popped open. The dirt road curved upward into nothingness. Cacti framed either side of it like gate posts from hell.

"Can't you go around?" she yelled just before they jettisoned off the edge.

"Yee ha," Bryce yelled, apparently regaining his confidence.

We're gonna die. Once again she got that roller coaster feeling in her stomach, and once again her helmet slipped down over her eyes. But the breeze was helping, enough so that she found herself wishing Bell helmets could fit up an editor's you-know-what.

"That wasn't so bad, was it?"

"I think I just wet my pants."

She heard chuckles and mustered up the strength to look over at him. Her head bounced against the seat as they flew over another bump, the cacti and rocks speeding by. He had a grin on his face, she could tell, even though his helmet obscured all but his cheeks and eyes.

"Now that's a first," he murmured. "I've never made a woman wet her pants without touching her."

Oh, jeez. Just what she needed, a randy wannabe race car driver making ribald jokes when she felt like death.

"Don't let it go to your head," she wheezed out, tilting her head again and inhaling a mouthful of dust.

"*How's it going out there, Bryce?*" Harry's voice crackled over the radio.

CJ groaned. Great, der Führer checking up on them.

Bryce pressed the button on his steering wheel, opening the connection to the radio. "We're doing fine...just fine."

Fine? Was the man living in another dimension? She gasped, dragging in more mouthfuls of grit.

Harry sounded equally incredulous...suspicious too. "*Uh huh,*" he said as if they'd told him they were pursuing a Russian submarine across the desert floor. "*And how's your passenger?*"

"She's doing just great, Harry. As a matter of fact, we were just talking about you."

"*You were?*"

"Yeah. I was relaying that story you'd told me about the time you lost control of your bodily functions and had to stop to change firesuits."

"*Damn it, Bryce, you didn't tell her that, did you?*"

Bryce darted her a glance and winked. "I sure did."

"*You son of a—*"

"What's the matter, Harry?" Bryce cut in. "I thought you'd want the world to know why it is Harry Santini wears brown firesuits."

"—*rip you out of that truck with my own two hands*," Harry continued, apparently unaware he'd been interrupted. "*And if you tell her one more—*"

"See you at the next stop, Harry," Bryce said, clicking the off switch.

CJ wanted to laugh, except she was afraid if she opened her mouth she'd start spewing something like the kid from *The Exorcist*. How the heck she was going to make it through the hour was beyond her. She should have listened to her mother and become a veterinarian. Sticking her arm up a horse's patootie had to be better than this.

"You didn't have to cover for me," she managed in a weak voice.

He stole another look at her. "Yeah, I did."

"Why?"

They flew over another bump, and CJ could feel the bruises forming on her rear.

"Because I admire you, CJ. And maybe if Harry thinks you handled this well, he'll let you ride the rest of the race."

CJ glanced at him, ignoring the flush of pleasure his words sent through her, and not at all sure how to tell him she wouldn't ride in this thing again if it meant the difference between a slow, horrific death and a fast, horrific death. But what the heck? She was probably in for slow and horrific anyway.

"Just out of curiosity, why are you doing this?" he asked again.

She debated telling him the truth, determined that thinking

took too much energy, and said, "My editor told me if I didn't cover this race he'd fire me."

He grew silent a moment. "That's kinda harsh."

"Yeah, well, Miles Van Dyke makes Norman Bates look like a choir boy."

He laughed again. "But you're supposed to ride along for the whole race."

Jeez, did he have to remind her? "Yup."

"Will your editor mind that you're not?"

"Do bears poop in the woods?" She looked into the distance. A bug committed suicide on the front window. Bug guts at a hundred miles an hour looked like somebody sneezed and forgot to wipe. Bile rose in her throat. She turned her head to the right again, hoping another view would settle her stomach. The sky was beautiful this time of morning. The browns, reds and golds of the desert dawn silhouetted the mountains, turning them into a color as pure as mahogany. It looked like rainbow sherbet. If she wasn't so close to barfing, she'd start singing "Oh What a Beautiful Morning".

"Maybe if you took some motion sickness pills?"

"Already did."

"Oh."

It was loud inside the truck, CJ noted, like being inside a barrel with a woodpecker banging on the outside.

"Damn...hold on."

She was beginning to hate those words. She looked ahead and grabbed the nearest thing to her, part of the roll cage. They careened, well, skidded really, around a bend to the right which, if taken at a normal speed, might not have been so bad. Taken at close to ninety, it felt like they were the end of a giant pendulum and the only thing holding them in was the racing harness.

"Good gracious," CJ huffed when they straightened out, her stomach doing triple toe loops.

"Yeah, I know. Sorry." The truck shook as they slammed into a pot hole the size of Crater Lake, then bounced back out. CJ almost bit her tongue off. As far as she was concerned, this hour was sixty minutes too long.

"Sorry. Missed that one too." He glanced at her, probably saw the crazed look in her eyes and said, "Did you know it was Harry's idea for me to do this?" in an obvious attempt to distract her.

No, she didn't. Did she care? Not really, though she probably should given her journalistic background.

"Just came up to me one day and said, 'I want you to do the Charity Pro/Am 2000'," Bryce continued as if he were on a Sunday drive, not sitting next to a woman terrified out of her skull and who was mentally composing her last will and testament. "I thought, sure, it'll be fun. Plus, it's for a good cause."

He glanced over at her again as they bounced in and then out of another pot hole.

"Harry and I go way back, but then I'm sure you know that. Anyway, a few weeks after Harry calls, he puts me behind the wheel of one of these things and I'm thinking, I can do this. I didn't know then about rock slides, deer smacking into your front grill, breaking down on the side of the road and getting bit by snakes. Hell, I thought it'd be fun."

"Snakes?" she gulped, her body tensing as they were flung into another turn.

"Yeah," Bryce said, the truck completely sideways. "Oops. Hold on."

Oops? The truck was sliding around like Herbie the Love Bug and all he had to say was *oops*? CJ tried not to gag as she grabbed for anything handy.

When they straightened out Bryce continued as if nothing had happened. "But it's the scorpions you've got to watch out for. At least you can hear the rattlers."

She was going to die. She just knew it. The truck skidded out. The tires found purchase. They shot ahead.

Bryce kept right on talking. "We fell into the river ten miles from our fifth re-fueling stop. That wasn't so bad, it was rolling over that scared the life out of me. Harry was scared too. Still, it could have been worse. As it was, it only knocked a few of Harry's teeth loose, but, heck, they were probably loose already. The water helped too. Always better to land on water than the desert floor. Harry says people sometimes roll their trucks on top of a bed of rattlers." He grew silent a moment, glancing her way to gauge her reaction.

"How long ago was that?" CJ managed to gasp.

"That was, let's see, about two months ago."

"You've only been practicing for two months?"

"Hey, don't worry. This course is easy. They make it that way so we won't kill ourselves."

How reassuring. "Do you like Harry?" she asked more to distract herself than any real interest.

"Harry? He's a great guy."

"Right," she said, which came out sounding like, "Rumph," because she'd suddenly been flung up out of her seat. She landed on her rear with another teeth cracking thud. Bryce didn't seem to notice.

"No. He is. Back when I owned a string of joke stores, I used to buy a lot of my gag gifts from him, then I decided to try my hand at selling kids toys, and, well, the rest is history."

She glanced at him. He had big, competent hands and they enveloped the steering wheel commandingly. The thought popped into her mind, unwanted, but there it was. *I wish those hands would competently envelope me.* And on the heels of that thought she wondered if that old wives' tale could be true...the one about a man's hands being as big as his...

"...Dick's," Bryce said. "It didn't go over too well."

"I beg your pardon." For one horrible moment she worried she might have spoken the words aloud.

"I said it was Dick's idea for me to carry some of Harry's more risqué items. We were together even back then."

She must have looked as confused as she was because he said, "Dick, you know, my Chief Executive Officer?"

She nodded, even though she didn't have a clue who he was talking about.

"Well, anyway, they didn't go over too well," he continued.

She didn't say anything, just tried to concentrate on maintaining her dignity.

"It was the Crotch Buster. One of those electric—"

"Don't," CJ said, holding up a weak hand. "I don't want to go there."

Bryce looked over at her, and CJ could see the wickedness in his eyes. Jeesh the man could grow plants with the heat of that gaze. But there was something else in those eyes too, like a curiosity of some sort.

"Why not?" he asked suggestively, watching her closely.

Good lord, the man could make her red, even as sick as she was. She turned away, her gaze fixing on a spot in the distance. *Professional, CJ. Be professional.* But not since the time her high school football team had stormed the girls' locker room had she blushed so much. Suddenly the one-ton truck seemed oppressive, about as small as a Matchbox. She glanced back at him. He was giving her that look, the look that seemed to say, "Wanna get lucky?" But of course that was ridiculous. Bryce wouldn't be interested in her. She had no doubt the man's bedpost looked like a totem pole with notches from top to bottom, notches earned from women who looked, well, not like her.

"Have you ever used one of Harry's Happy Toys?"

"I beg your pardon?"

He smiled. At least she thought he smiled. Hard to tell with the helmet on, but the corners of his eyes crinkled again.

"A happy toy, you know. One of—"

"Mr. Danvers," she interrupted. "Please, do we need to have this conversation?"

"Yes. And the name's Bryce."

She slanted him a glance designed to make him think of schoolmarms and Catholic schools.

"C'mon. Tell me. Have you?"

She would not answer. She *would not answer.*

"I promise not to tell anyone if you have."

"Shouldn't you keep your eyes on the road?"

He shrugged, focusing ahead again. "Not going to answer, eh? Too bad. And, no, I don't need to look at the road. There are two things I'm naturally great at; driving is the other one."

"Oh, really," she replied tartly. Something caught her attention. She glanced forward, then suddenly stiffened. "Is that why you're about to hit that cactus?"

"What cactus?" He faced forward. "Da—!"

CJ closed her eyes. Time to die.

Bryce hit the brakes. CJ jerked forward in her seat. The sound of tires scrubbing the desert floor filled the cabin.

"Oh man," CJ moaned.

It was like being on the teacup ride at Disneyland.

A long while later silence descended round them. Dust, bits of debris, and the smell of burnt tires filled the cab. CJ waved her hand in front of her face as her heart slowly, reluctantly resumed its normal pace.

It was a while before she felt strong enough to say, "Nice going, Bryce."

"I meant to do that."

She arched a brow.

He met her gaze, and despite his brave words she could see the residue of fear in his eyes. "I was trying to demonstrate my driving skill."

"Skill, huh? Is that what you call it?"

"Like I said, driving's the other thing I do well."

"And how many people have you almost killed in bed?" The comment slipped out, unprofessional, but gone before she could retrieve it.

He leaned toward her, and CJ's heart began to beat like a twenty-one gun salute.

"They've had to call the paramedics on more than one occasion."

She knew he was joking. Knew he was just trying to assert his male ego after almost turning them into road kill. But she didn't care. He was still the sexiest thing who had ever flirted with her, and he *was* flirting with her, no doubt about it, though why was beyond her. Probably out of pity.

Despite the disappointing thought, adrenaline surged through her body and made an immediate dive to her private parts. She glanced over her shoulder. No back seat. Darn.

Knock it off, Ceej. He's just jerking your chain. Don't let him see you panting. Men like him are never serious. At least not about women like you.

"Tell me, Bryce, have you always had such a big ego? Or are you just a legend in your own mind?"

He ignored the last bit and said softly, "I'd like to know you." He shifted closer. "Intimately."

Lordy, Lordy, the man was Trouble. Pure, unadulterated reckless trouble. She squirmed in her seat. "Dream on," said her mouth. *In your wet dreams,* screamed her mind. But man, oh man, did she wish he was serious.

"Oh, it'd be no dream."

"You're right. It'd be a nightmare."

Strangely enough, her comment made him hoot out loud. The sound sent chills down her spine. And then he looked at her and gave her that bad-boy smile.

"And here I thought you didn't like me."

"Oh, I never said I didn't like you. I just wish I'd drawn Tim Allen to race with instead."

He moved even closer. CJ resisted the urge to draw away. "You wouldn't want to race with that guy."

His words whispered across her face. "Why not?" she asked hoarsely.

"Because my tools are *way* bigger."

Chapter Three

Bryce waited for her reaction, laughter hovering. Gosh, she was adorable. Her eyes had actually widened a bit at the word tool.

"The men I date don't have to use those to keep *me* happy."

He laughed. Couldn't help himself.

"Not that they ever *care* if I'm happy," she mumbled morosely.

His laughter faded.

She must have recognized her mistake. Green eyes shot to his. Color filled her cheeks.

"Please tell me you didn't hear that."

"Hear what?" he said too late.

She leaned her head against her seat and groaned. "You *did* hear it."

"No, I didn't."

"Liar."

Yes, he was, but past experience had taught a wise man always denies a woman's accusations.

"Look. Just forget I said it, 'kay? Men treat me just fine."

Ah huh. And he was Mr. Rogers. He didn't know how he knew it, but he did.

"Terrific."

Horrible.

"Like a queen."

They chewed up her heart, spat it out and trod on it, he could tell. Maybe it was the way she reacted to his flirting, like she wanted to flirt back, but didn't trust him to play nice. She'd been wounded. And he knew exactly how she felt. Oh, women didn't treat him like that now. He made sure of it. But back before he was a big successful business man? Oh, yeah. These days he didn't let them get close. Love 'em and leave 'em. That was his motto.

"Can you start the car?"

"Truck," he corrected.

"Whatever."

But he didn't. Instead he found himself placing a hand on her leg.

She jumped. Eyes darted to his.

"Not all men are pigs."

She raised a brow. "Just the ones who keep me company, present company excluded, of course."

"Of course." He removed his hand, but Bryce knew behind the bluster, behind the bravado, embarrassment hovered. She couldn't hide it. He had the feeling CJ couldn't hide much with that pixie face of hers. Kinda cute and endearing, that face.

Which is why he said, "If it helps, I've been treated pretty rotten too."

"You?" she scoffed. "What? Did a woman actually say no to you once upon a time?"

The comment stung, which was odd. It wasn't any worse than one of his buddies had said before.

"Oh, man," she mumbled.

He searched for the keys to the truck, remembered he needed to push a button, and raised a hand.

She stayed him, her warm fingers covering his. "Look," she said, green eyes soft. "I'm sorry. That was really rude. You were trying to be nice. I mean, sure, you're the Playboy Prankster, but you're also a man. It's possible you could have been hurt a time or two."

More than possible. Really, *really* possible. Before Toyco, women had treated him like a big brother. Cute, but not someone you'd ever marry. Sure all that had changed, but hell, he still remembered what hurting felt like. Lana the Lesbian, Harry'd dubbed his ex-fiancée. The words stabbed every time.

"Obviously, you got over it. Just like I've gotten over my bad relationships."

Yup. He'd gotten over Lana. Didn't think about her at all. Nah ah. Not ever.

"But we don't need to discuss our personal lives. In fact, we should probably get going."

Yeah, they probably should, except her fingers felt nice on his hand.

"How much longer do we have, by the way?"

She was so natural. No goo on her face. No fufu hair color. No neon nails. Just CJ. "Forty-five minutes."

She looked disappointed.

"Don't worry, it'll go quick."

"Oh yeah?"

She was a Chevy, he admitted. Plain exterior. Big engine. His gaze caught on her breasts. Big engines.

"Relax. I'll take care of you." He clasped her hand in his own.

She looked startled. Their eyes met. Something clicked.

"You know what?" he said softly.

"What?" the word barely a whisper.

"You have dust all over your face."

"Wh—" She drew back. "Oh."

Bryce wanted to kick himself. Now why'd he have to go and do that?

"Is it gone?"

He'd spoiled a perfect moment. "Yeah." But he knew why he'd done it. This feeling he had whenever he stared at her, it did funny thing to his insides. Things that should be avoided at all costs. After Lana, Bryce had vowed to steer clear of serious relationships, no matter how sweetly adorable a woman might appear.

"Thanks," she said.

Too bad he had a feeling he was about to break his own rule.

Forty minutes later CJ wanted to die. Unfortunately, she hadn't yet.

"How much longer?" she gasped.

"Shouldn't be too much."

They raced ahead, the truck scattering a flurry of sand and dust in their wake. Bryce had been quiet since their little one-on-one. That bothered her, especially since he kept glancing at her, frowning, then turning away. He must regret allowing her to come along. Not surprising since *she* regretted going, especially since she'd had the silly urge to kiss him back there...

"Tell CJ she's got one minute to leave the truck." Harry's voice crackled over the radio.

Thoughts of kissing Bryce, and his not wanting to kiss her, scattered. "I've got how long?" she gaped.

"One minute," Bryce repeated.

"He's joking, right?"

"Nope."

She'd been afraid he'd say that. Impossible. It would take one minute for her stomach to settle, much less figure out the seat belts. She looked heavenward, and asked God why She'd suddenly taken it upon Herself to desert her in this hour of need. She was a good girl; always paid her parking tickets, allowed little old ladies to cross the street, never slept with a guy on the first date. Heck, not even the fifth date, not that anyone had asked in a while...a long while.

"I'll help you out if you like."

Ha! That was the last thing she needed. Having Bryce touch her was like being jolted with a cattle prod. But at least a cattle prod's sting went away. She could *still* feel where his fingers had stroked her own. No, thank you, she didn't need to make a fool of herself any more than she already had.

"I can manage," she said with more confidence than she felt.

Five minutes later they careered to a halt in front of the Star Oil transporter. Bryce cut the motor instantly. The silence was as startling as being plunged naked into a pool of water. Harry stood by a group of men all dressed exactly alike, a red star imprinted on the front of their black shirts. Each of them stared at the truck like it held the last cup of water in the whole wide world. A man rushed forward with a dump can of fuel.

Harry's voice boomed over the radio. *"Get out of the truck,*

CJ."

Put your hands on top of your head. You have the right to remain silent.

But at least fugitives had longer than a minute, she thought disgustedly. They also had access to an item CJ would give her word processor to possess, a door handle. She looked forward to crawling out the window about as much as she would a tonsillectomy. But first she had to release the darn net thingy. "How does it come off?"

Bryce cleared his throat. "First, you should start with the zipper."

CJ's hands paused on the nylon web. "Do you mind," she huffed. "I'm in a hurry." She turned back to window. "The *net*. How do I get the *safety* net off?" she asked, fiddling with the catches.

"Oh, the *net*. Just slide it to the right."

She should smack him. She really should. She did as instructed, relieved when the darn net slid free. Her seat belts came next, actually easier to undo than she'd thought. Unfortunately, her exit strategy was the next problem. If she went belly first then she'd slide blindly to the desert floor face first, and with her luck, probably land on it too. If she went feet first, she'd have to do it on her belly, and give the world outside a fine view of the world's largest rear end in the process. Feet first, she thought. Dignity be damned.

She moved toward the window, her head suddenly jerking back.

"Helps if you take off the helmet and disconnect those ear pieces."

"Right." CJ fumed silently. He was enjoying this, the pinhead. Feeling every second slip by, she pulled off the helmet; cool air rushed over her face. Great. She probably looked as bad as Tina Turner on a good hair day. Her editor was going to pay for this, and it was going to be a slow, arduous death.

Gingerly, she pushed herself up so that she crouched on the seat, then turned and sat on the sill of the window facing Bryce. She gave him an Eat Doo-Doo and Die look, moved one leg, then the other out the window, her arms the only thing holding her in the truck. Slowly she tried to slide down.

Nothing happened.

She released a little more of her weight.

Still nothing.

She released a lot more weight.

Nothing. Nada. Zip.

She could, in fact, feel where her firesuit had snagged on the safety net. She looked up to see Bryce trying to contain his laughter.

"Well, don't just sit there, help me."

Then he did something she would never forgive him for; he threw his head back and laughed so hard CJ was tempted to toss something at him, except she couldn't move. He released his helmet and earpieces. It was no comfort whatsoever that his dark hair looked like the spines of a porcupine, nor that his handsome face was as flushed as her own after he'd pulled off the helmet. She was too busy mentally ticking off the seconds she wasted by hanging half in, half out the dang window.

Bryce leaned toward her.

And suddenly CJ was aware only of the most fantastic pair of eyes she'd ever seen. They were beautiful—like liquid turquoise—only with blues and grays and greens and laughter all mixed in. Those eyes never left hers as he leaned closer...and closer still, until he was only micrometers away.

CJ tensed. He stared at her for a long moment. She held

her breath as he bent his dark head; the caress of his hands on her waist was like the touch of a laser. She closed her eyes and tried to control the ra-tap-tap of her heart. He smelled like a forest after a summer rain. Great, she thought. She probably smelled like Mrs. O'Leary's cow.

"You're caught on the net."

"I know."

"Just move a little to your right."

She did.

"Wow."

CJ tensed. Her eyes sprung open. "Oh, man, what's wrong?"

He looked up, his lips only inches away. "You have nice breasts."

At that moment something pinged, something ripped, something split. Down she went, sliding toward the desert floor like Fred Flintstone, sans the dinosaur tail. She landed with an oomph.

The men in her immediate vicinity started to laugh, Harry, no doubt, one of them. She took a moment to catch her breath. Gingerly sat up. Bryce hung his head out the passenger side window; one arm rested on the sill ostensibly to see if she was okay, but in reality to gauge her reaction to the nice breasts comment, CJ was sure. She'd like to wipe that sexy grin right off his face with a twenty pound eraser.

Trouble. No doubt about it.

The belief doubled when he said, "Gee, CJ, *you* have big tools too."

Chapter Four

"I'm not leaving without her, Harry."

Harry Santini looked ready to spit piston rings. "What do you mean you won't leave without her?"

Bryce smiled down at him, the same smile he'd used on Harry for more than one business deal. "I mean it, Harry."

"Did she put you up to this?" He jammed a thumb over his shoulder toward CJ, who sat on the bumper of the transporter about fifty yards away, the big rig dwarfing her. The helmet she'd discarded lay at her feet. She looked ready to vomit.

"She doesn't even know I'm asking you, Harry."

"*She doesn't know?*"

Bryce studied his watch. "We're losing time."

"Don't tell me that, you dang idiot. If we're losing time, it's your own fault." Harry clutched the clipboard in his hand like he wanted to bash him over the head with it. "You were supposed to take off again ten minutes ago."

"Go get her, Harry."

"Damn it, Bryce. Give me one good reason why I should."

"She has nice breasts."

Harry's eyes bulged, and for the first time Bryce noted Harry bore a striking resemblance to Rodney Dangerfield, especially when he was in the midst of a really good rage, like right now.

"She has nice breasts," Harry muttered. He tilted his head back toward the sky. "She has nice breasts?" he repeated, then pinned Bryce with a glare. "So?"

Bryce looked over at CJ. She stared at them, no doubt wondering why they hadn't left the staging area. "I like women with nice breasts, Harry."

"I've seen you with plenty of women with bigger jugs than hers, but you never looked at them the way you're looking at her."

Did he look at her differently? That gave him pause, especially coming after their little heart-to-heart. But he'd only had that little chat to take her mind off her motion sickness, he reassured himself, not because he was interested in her or anything. He liked his life just the way it was: Nice, heterosexual women when he wanted. No fuss. No muss. Even if there was something about CJ that appealed to him. Maybe it was that lost puppy look in her eyes. Yeah, that was it.

"She needs us, Harry. That editor of hers sounds like a real jerk. First he conned you into thinking she was a man, and now she tells me if she doesn't do a good job, she'll get fired."

That got Harry's attention. One thing never changed about Harry Santini. He had a heart of gold, which was how Harry had known Bryce would agree to drive his million dollar race truck in the name of charity.

Harry darted a glare in CJ's direction, then looked down at his stop watch. When he scowled back up at him, Bryce knew he'd won. One other thing about Harry, he wanted to win. It didn't matter if it was a race or a game of Monopoly, the man liked the thrill of victory...and he wanted to be the victor of the Charity Pro/Am 2000.

"I'm going to regret this," Harry said. "I just know I am."

"You're a prince, Harry.'

"Yeah? Tell it to my ex-wife."

"Wives, Harry. It's ex-wives."

"Whatever." He turned and started to stomp away; a small gust of hot desert wind rustled the papers on his clipboard.

"Oh, and Harry?"

Harry stopped, then slowly turned to face him.

"Tell her to take more motion sickness pills.

"*Motion sickness?*" Harry roared. "She gets motion sick?"

Bryce started the truck. He could see Harry's mouth open and shut like the flaps of an exhaust valve. Never mind Harry, he thought, tightening the strap of his helmet. He'd calm down. And it'd be great to have some company along for the ride.

That was why he'd done it, he told himself. Not because he was interested in CJ or anything. Nope. Not his type. He preferred women with a little more pizzazz. A little more zing. Women who were, well, womanly.

He looked back at CJ. She watched Harry approach with a wary look in her eyes.

"He wants me to *what?*"

"He wants you ride alongside of him for the rest of the day."

That's what CJ thought he'd said. She narrowed her eyes, studying Harry's face intently. He didn't *look* like he had heat stroke. Still, looks could be deceiving.

"Why?"

Harry grew flustered. Not surprising since he had a truck idling like it was in the middle of the Santa Monica freeway.

"I dunno why. But he told me to tell you he's not leaving without you."

Bryce not leaving without her? Ha! Still, it was a nice gesture. He probably thought he did her a favor, but she wanted to ride in that truck again about as much as she wanted a leg amputated.

"Gee, Harry, tell Bryce that's really sweet, but I think I'll pass."

Harry didn't take the news well. At all. His forehead dripped with sweat. His face got as red as the mammoth-sized toolbox sitting next to them. He didn't look healthy. In fact, CJ was about to suggest a low fat, low cholesterol diet when he suddenly said, "He told me you have nice breasts."

At first the comment didn't register.

"Said they were real nice. Plump," Harry went on, shoving his clipboard under one arm, then cupping his hands like he tested the weight of melons. "Like this."

CJ stared up at him in dismay.

"He. Said. What?"

Slowly she pushed to her feet, her sore body trembling.

"He said—"

"Never. Mind." She raised her hands and cut him off mid stream. She turned away.

"Where're you going?"

"To tell him he can kiss my bruised and battered derriere."

"In front of the fans?"

She paused, looked at the various faces milling around them. The smell of exhaust hung on the air, the big rigs lined up with their back facing each other like gunfighters in a stand-off, but didn't seem to dissuade the people who'd arrived to watch the Celebrity Pro/Am 2000.

She put on the brakes, then turned back to face him. "You're right. Give me those." She reached for the headset resting around his neck.

"Now hold on a minute," Harry said, moving it before she could snatch it away. "Maybe you shouldn't use these."

"Why not?"

"Because if you do, every person listening in on this frequency will know all about it...just like they heard him tell me you had nice breasts."

What? Then she remembered. Radio frequencies the teams used were common knowledge. Quite a number of people listened in on the conversations between driver and crew. Officials. Fans. Sponsors. You never knew what you might hear, like somebody saying a woman had nice breasts.

She wanted to choke Bryce.

No, wait, she wanted to castrate him.

It was one thing to make a comment about breasts in the privacy of your own race truck, quite another to share it with the rest of Western civilization. And what if Miles-the-Editor-from-Hell heard about it? Oh man, what if Miles thought she and Bryce were... Or what if he didn't, but still used it as an excuse to send her packing? And if she got fired again she could kiss her journalistic career good-bye. She wouldn't let that happen...*couldn't* let that happen. Even if it meant climbing back into that four wheeled gas chamber and riding along just to prove to Miles what a darn good reporter she was.

Not giving Harry a backward glance, she pushed her way through the fans to get to the starting line. Just her luck that a camera crew turned their lenses upon her when she approached. No doubt they, too, wondered why the children's toy store tycoon hadn't taken off.

"Hey, lady, do you belong here?" asked a lanky official dressed in, of all colors, dirt-enhancing white.

"Yup," she nodded, pointing to the truck. "I'm the boobs riding along with Danvers."

The man bit back a smile and waved her through. Terrific. All the officials must have heard too. Just terrific.

Bryce spotted her, revving the motor, the truck emitting a puff of white smoke potent enough to make birds drop out of the sky. Out the corner of her eye she saw the cameraman step closer. Great. Just what she needed. Now her rump would be broadcast on the evening news, probably with some ditzy blonde saying, "The moon made a sudden appearance over the Nevada Desert today. But what was originally thought to be an *ass*-tral phenomenon turned out to be journalist CJ Randall..."

"Need some help?" offered Harry, who'd followed her.

Did she need help making a fool of herself? Of course she didn't. Getting into the truck was the problem. Darn thing was as big as a tank and the only way in it was with the help of a crane, a catapult or a hefty pair of hands. Earlier, she'd had a step ladder. No such luck now. She just hoped she didn't throw old Harry's back out when he lifted her up to the sill. But first she looked through the open window, took careful aim at Bryce's head, then threw her helmet at his handsome face. It bounced off his helmet with a clunk.

"Hey!" she saw him mouth.

Childish, yes, but boy did it feel good. Show *that* on the evening news.

She faced Harry again, motioning him forward since talking was pointless. Officials kept the crowd from getting too close. A second truck pulled up behind them, the noise of the two trucks combined deafening. If the CIA ever wanted a sure-fire way to keep their conversations under wraps, they could hold their top secret meetings next to a race truck. She'd need a hearing aid by the time this was all over.

As it turned out it would have been simpler if she *had* used a crane. It took not only Harry but Bryce tugging on her from the inside to get her in, the camera whirring away as it captured her humiliation for the six o'clock news and an Off Road Racing Bloopers tape. Fortunately her firesuit didn't snag as she tumbled headfirst into the cockpit.

"Why in the *hell* doesn't this thing have door handles?" She didn't care that she'd broken her cardinal rule not to swear. She was in a swearin' mood, dang it. Just right now all she wanted to do was push herself into a sitting position, give Bryce a piece of her mind, and somehow make it through the next hour of purgatory.

She connected herself to the radio, then shoved her borrowed helmet over her head. "You'd think these people would at least be able to do that."

"What?" Bryce asked in her ear.

She glowered at him and said, "Pick someone to drive who has a brain."

"Hey," he said, his dark brow rising. "What'd I do?"

"For one thing you forced me to ride in this truck again."

A black brow arched. "I'm not forcing you to do anything. I thought you'd be pleased."

"Yeah, well, I'm jumping for joy, can't you tell? But that's not what's really bothering me. What's really bothering me is you told God and everybody you like my breasts."

"I do."

CJ frowned.

"Really," Bryce added, and dang it if he didn't look serious.

Delight surged through her. She squashed it down like a bug. "Listen, buster. You may think your comments are cute, but I've got a career on the line here. If my editor hears about your fetish for my breasts, he's going to think the worst."

"Worst?"

"Yeah, the worst."

"What's the worst?"

"That...well, you know."

He gave her a deliberately blank stare. And why did she think she saw that wicked gleam in his eyes? But two could play that game.

She leaned close to him, as close as her radio leash would allow, then placed her hand on his thigh, for added effect, she told herself, but in reality he see if it felt as good as it looked; hard and taut. Yup.

His blue eyes narrowed.

"He'll think I've screwed your brains out."

The truck lurched, then stalled. CJ bit back a laugh. Served the jerk right.

"*What happened?*" Harry screamed.

"We're fine, Harry. My foot just slipped off the clutch."

Silence. The buzz of the radio, then Harry's irritated voice, "*Thought you blew the freakin' motor.*" She could hear the deep breath he took. "*Listen, the timer will let you go in a sec. So far you're thirteen minutes behind the leader.*"

"Roger, Harry." Bryce turned to look at her, starting the motor at the same time. "That was a raunchy thing to say."

She pursed her lips in puritanical fashion. "You deserved it."

"I like raunchy women."

"I bet you do."

"And I've never made love to a woman in a truck before."

She tilted her head at him. "Oh yeah? Couldn't squeeze it

in, huh?"

He gave her a sly look.

She raised her hand. "No, no, no, no. Do *not* make a comment about squeezing things in. I know where you want to go with that and I refuse to follow."

She heard him laugh softly. Jeez. Did the man have no shame? And did he have to make her want to laugh too? Her anger at him had slowly dissipated, leaving behind the awareness she'd felt from the moment she'd met him, an awareness that doubled when she'd touched him. Her firesuit had just about melted right off her overheated body.

"Look this conversation is going nowhere—"

"We could make it go somewhere," he said flirtatiously.

"Stop it," she ordered, hoping the helmet hid her blush.

His expression seemed to say, "But why?"

"Look, you and I both know I'm not your type—"

"You're not?"

She rolled her eyes. "No. My waist size isn't the same as my IQ." Good lord, had she really said such a catty thing out loud?

He laughed, the sound of it startling.

Apparently, she had.

He had one of those laughs that was deep and rich and utterly masculine. Her heart lurched, then resumed beating at a furious rate. There was a look in his eyes, one she didn't recognize.

"Who cares about your waist size?"

"I do," she answered warily.

"You shouldn't."

"Oh?"

"You have other attributes."

"Like what?" Okay, so she was fishing for compliments. Who cared?

"Your eyes."

Don't let the compliment go to your head, Ceej. Trouble, remember?

"I like the way they glitter when you're mad."

"Jennifer Haynes."

He blinked. "Huh?"

"You dated her for a year. Said the same thing about *her* eyes."

His brows rose. "How'd you know that?"

She shifted in her seat. "I read it in my research."

"Well, you have prettier hair than she does. Brown, with a hint of—"

"Autumn fire," she finished for him.

He looked genuinely horrified. "And how'd you know that?"

"Easy. It's a favorite saying of yours. Used it to describe one of your Irish Setters."

He looked speechless.

"There're tons of articles about you, you know. TV clips too. 'America's most eligible bachelor'," she mimicked. "The toy store tycoon. I spent a whole week going through it all."

He glanced at her again, and for a second she thought he was about to say something, but he didn't.

"Want me to tell you what I learned?"

He didn't answer.

She filled him in anyway. "You like kids, fast cars and anything in a tight skirt. You don't like men who beat women— a point in your favor—but you think women with careers are a social calamity, a point *not* in your favor. You're a notorious flirt. Have a girlfriend in every city and prefer blondes over brunettes." She smiled. "On the other hand, you don't drink, have a brilliant mind and a wicked sense of humor. You love animals, country music and cooking flamboyant dinners for your many dates. In fact, you'd be perfect husband material except for the fact that you've sworn never to marry. Have I got it right?"

Bryce didn't say a word. His blue eyes stared into hers. She could see the little hamster wheel in his mind spinning madly.

Then his eyes narrowed.

Uh oh.

He leaned toward her.

Double uh oh.

"All except the part about career women," he answered, placing his hand on her thigh. "I like them just fine."

Her heart stopped. Yeah, right. He was just trying to save face. Obviously, her character sketch had hit a little too close to home. "Don't play games with me."

He stroked her thigh. "Why not?"

She shoved his hand away. "Because I'm a professional."

"Professional what?" He touched her again.

"Shuttle pilot," she snapped sarcastically, shoving his hand away again. "Reporter, you nimrod, what else?"

He chuckled, leaning away from her, which was a relief, or so CJ told herself.

"You know something, CJ, I enjoy baiting you. You make me laugh."

"Yeah, well, I once made Ted Bundy laugh too, but that didn't change who he was inside."

"Bundy! You're comparing me to Bundy?"

"Why not? You're both lady killers."

He drew back.

She smiled. As hits go, it wasn't all that bad, and it had the desired effect.

"You really don't like me, do you?" And he sounded surprised, maybe even hurt. Okay, so maybe she was a little hard on him. Maybe that's why she found herself being unusually snarky when around him. But she needed to be. She had to keep him at a distance, had to keep it professional, because if she didn't, well, she didn't want to delve into what would happen if she let her body rule her actions.

"I didn't say I don't like you. You're just...not my type."

"Is that a challenge?"

She rolled her eyes. The man just wouldn't stop. "Look, can we change the subject?"

"Sure. What'd you want to talk about?"

"How you're going to tell Harry you lied about seeing my breasts."

Snap. Back came the flirt.

"But I wasn't lying. I also saw your pink lace bra."

Oh *greeeat.*

"Do you have matching panties on too?"

It amazed her the way the sound of his voice could make her body flush, make her squirm in her seat, make her skin tingle.

"*You'll* never know," she said as firmly as she could. Her heart pounded. The pulse point on her neck throbbed. His next comment almost had her in cardiac arrest.

"I'd like to know."

Easy, Ceej, a little voice warned. *He's not serious. He's just trying to make you squirm. You called him a notorious flirt, and now he's showing you just how notorious he can be. And even if he were serious, you can't risk your job by becoming one of Bryce's gal pals.*

"Don't get your hopes up," she said more to herself than to him.

"*Ahh, Bryce, would you mind paying attention? The starter said he's going to disqualify you if you don't go through the timer within the next thirty seconds.*" Harry's frustration came through loud and clear over the radio. They both looked up in time to see an official waving a green flag.

"In a minute, Harry."

"*A minute. Damn it, Bryce, we don't have a min—*"

Bryce clicked the off switch; Harry's voice abruptly disappeared. He turned to her. "Put your harness on."

Her harness. Shoot. She'd almost forgotten. Her stomach lurched. The realization that she was about to bounce around on her tush again filled her with as much enthusiasm as having a rectal exam.

It must have showed on her face because Bryce said, "I asked one of Harry's crew to put some motion sickness pills in the first aid kit, so if you haven't taken any more, you can take one now. I can hold off for a sec."

She glanced at him, telling herself not to be affected by his thoughtfulness, but it was hard. Just when you worked yourself up to not to like a guy, he went and did something sweet. And though she hadn't mentioned it to him, that was something her research had revealed too. Bryce Danvers was famous for doing nice things, like taking customers on shopping sprees. Supplying children's toys to homeless shelters. Or racing a truck across the desert to raise money for critically ill children. He was a one-in-a-million man, but she'd never be his one-in-a-million lady, she reminded herself. Men didn't see her that way. They saw her as a plain, slightly overweight gal. Someone to fool around with until something better came along. Bryce just toyed with her to pass the time. She could see it in his eyes, even if it hurt her to admit it.

Face it, Ceej. You have about as much chance catching his attention as you do catching a star. Just remember what happened with Ed.

Ed.

The news desk's hottest reporter at her last job. Handsome. Smart. And a big flirt, too. She'd been flattered when he'd asked her out, had thought that maybe she'd finally found a man who could look past her full figure and plain exterior. But then one of the story ideas she'd been secretly working on had turned up on the front page under his byline. And she, the queen of naive, had believed him when he'd told her it was all an accident. And then it'd happened again and CJ had come to the bitter conclusion that she was being used. When she'd confronted Ed all hell had broken loose. Nasty accusations had been hurled, and because she was the new kid on the block, she'd been fired when she'd gone to her editor. Later, she'd heard it was Ed who'd accused *her* of stealing *his* ideas. Unbelievable.

"Reach behind the seat if you're interested. There's a squeeze bottle of water in there too."

"Thanks." She should have learned her lesson then. Trouble was *not* to be trusted.

The kit was right where he said it'd be, a white box emblazoned with an Avon Red Cross. She would take the whole bottle. Maybe then she wouldn't feel as miserable. The first ever comatose reporter, but what the heck. A drug-induced story would most definitely be more entertaining to read...and probably write. She pressed the button.

The box exploded.

Well, not the box, exactly. It was what was inside that blew up...and up...and up...the center of it inflating at a rate of speed on par with a 747's escape ramp.

"What the hell—" Bryce yelled.

It must be a life raft, but how in the heck she'd triggered the darn thing was beyond her, and what was a life raft doing inside a first aid box? An odd shaped raft, at that. It had cones sticking out of it, cones with red bull's eyes in the center.

And that's when it hit her.

It was *not* a life raft.

"It's a Joceline in the Box," Bryce pronounced on a laugh. "Harry's self-inflating blow up doll."

"What's it doing in my lap?" she squeaked.

Bryce laughed. "Harry told me the crew likes to booby-trap the truck every now and then."

Booby being the operative word. Terrific. Just what she needed, a bunch of pranksters making her life hell, as if she didn't have her hands full already.

She tried to shove the thing out the window, but forgot about the net. It bounced right off with a hollow thunk. The thing was all arms and legs now, a life-sized rendition of Pink Pumps with painted blonde hair and Morticia eye makeup. She tried to maneuver it toward Bryce, who, by now, was laughing uncontrollably.

"Unplug the air valve," he offered, his words barely understandable. The doll's head was in Bryce's lap, face down, it's big inflated behind bouncing just beneath CJ's nose.

She wanted to die.

Outside, Harry's crew, all five of them, doubled over. The crowd of spectators standing around were laughing too.

Everyone was chuckling, except for Harry. He was too busy glancing from his stop watch, to the truck, to the white-clad official, to the truck, to his stop watch, to the white-clad official...

His face turned redder as he furiously waved them forward. She saw his mouth move, and she didn't need a radio to know he screamed at them to go, go, go.

"Finish putting your harness on, CJ," Bryce choked out, apparently having read Harry's lips too.

Get a hold of yourself, Ceej. Now was not the time for an emotional outburst. She fumbled with the doll, unexpected and unwanted tears clouding her eyes.

Why was she crying?

"Hurry."

"I can't. She's in the way."

Her frustration mounted as she tried to shove the plastic doll to the floor, but one of its breasts got caught on the steering wheel. There wasn't enough room to shove her under the dash, either.

"Here, let me help."

Bryce picked the thing up, ducking beneath it to help her secure the myriad of belts. A leg sailed over the back of CJ's head, the other obstructing her vision. Bryce's hands fumbled around; she heard the distinct click of the belts. When he straightened, he took one look at her and roared with fresh laughter. It was only as she gazed at him across an expanse of beige, plastic flesh that she understood why.

The doll was facing up now, its conical-shaped breasts pointing gloriously to the headliner, a leg on either side of her head. It was obscene...it was disgusting. It was...

"Hilarious," Bryce supplied.

Chapter Five

But she didn't look like she thought it was hilarious, Bryce noted. In fact, she looked distinctly like a woman he'd once pinched, right before she'd slapped him. Funny. He'd have thought CJ the type to enjoy a good joke as much as he.

"Get it out of here," she sniffed.

He reached for the doll, wondering what the heck had gotten in to her. Gone was the little pistol who'd analyzed his life with such cutting sarcasm. In her place sat a woman who looked distinctly like she was…"You're crying," he accused.

"No, I'm not," she huffed.

But he'd been around women long enough to know blotchy complexions went along with teary eyes.

"You're crying," he accused.

Someone pounded on the door. Harry.

"Damn it," his long-time friend screamed through the net. "Get your butt out there."

"In a minute, Harry. CJ's crying."

"She's what?"

"No, I'm not," CJ protested.

"Yes, you are."

"Why's she crying?" from Harry.

"I don't know."

"I'm not crying," CJ all but yelled.

"Must be the prank the boys pulled," Bryce surmised.

"It's not the prank," she moaned. "It's...it's...PMS."

Bryce drew back.

Harry said, "See ya."

CJ looked away.

Harry had the right idea. PMS? Great. "Do you need some aspirin or something?"

"I need a life," he thought he heard her moan. Not a good sign. Especially when it came from the mouth of a woman experiencing a hormonal imbalance.

"Look, if this is about that prank, don't think anything of it. The boys are always—"

"It's not that," she sniffed. "Oh, gosh, I can't *believe* this is happening to me."

"What? That you're crying?"

She turned a look upon him, a look men the world over recognized and feared. "I am not crying."

"Okay, so you're not crying. Tell me why you're not laughing at what was—" he patted the doll's bottom, "—a very good prank."

She didn't answer.

"I know you have a sense of humor."

"Oh, yeah?" She stiffened suddenly, then quickly reached for the doll. A second later she'd popped the plug, the doll instantly deflating.

"Does that make you feel better?"

Her look clearly said, "Do I look like I feel better?" And she didn't, he admitted, she still looked upset. Sad even. He mulled that over for a second before she waved an imperious hand and said, "Let's go."

But he didn't want to go. Oddly enough, he wanted to soothe her just like he had earlier. He stiffened, his foot almost slipping off the gas again. What was wrong with him?

Too much sun.

"Well?" she asked, arching a brow.

But, danged if he didn't like her spunk. All the women he knew would be ranting and raving at the prank just pulled on her. In fact, some of them had ranted and raved at the jokes he'd pulled on *them*. But not CJ. Oh, sure, she wasn't exactly thrilled, but that was probably the hormones. No wonder she'd looked a little green earlier. And yet not once had she complained about it. Nor had she complained about her hair, breaking a nail, or getting dirty. The most she'd done was get a little emotional just now. What a gal.

"Br-yce," Harry's irritated voice screamed through the net.

He turned to look at his friend, feeling kinda weird suddenly.

"If you're not going to drive the damn truck, then get out and let *me* drive."

"Right, Harry," he murmured, pressing the gas pedal. But he didn't floor it, no, he sorta strolled past the starting line.

"*Dammit, Bryce—*" he heard Harry scream, before they were out of range.

"What are you doing?" CJ asked warily.

"Takin' it easy until you feel better." He shot her a reassuring smile. "Let me know if you get crampy or anything."

Her eyes widened, before they looked a bit...guilty? "Thanks."

He stared at her a second longer, realized he must've been

imagining it and said, "Sure."

"And I wasn't crying," she reiterated.

"I know. You probably had some dirt in your eyes or something."

He could see her nod out of the corner of his eye.

"Yeah. Dirt."

He shot her another glance. She was nibbling her bottom lip. "You know you really are a good sport."

She didn't look at him. Bryce didn't know if that was good or bad.

"And don't mind the crew. They're just treating you like one of the guys."

This time she turned toward him. "One of the guys. Is that all I am, just one of the boys?"

Uh oh. Times like these were like navigating a mine field. You never knew when something would blow up in your face.

"Hey. Don't take that wrong. It's a compliment. If you were any other woman, they'd have never done what they did."

"Any other woman being svelte and glamorous and perfect."

Oh, man. Things were going from bad to worse. "That's not what I meant."

"What *do* you mean?"

He thought about it for a moment, toyed with flooring it so he could end the conversation, and the hole he'd dug for himself, and ended up saying, "I mean you're not like the other women I've seen hanging out at the races. You've got moxy. Hell, I doubt any of them know someone who'd have the nerve to ride along in one of these things. But not only have you done it once, now you're back to do it again. You've got guts, and to top it all off, the prettiest eyes I've ever seen. I'm sure the crew has noticed that too."

There. She couldn't possibly misinterpret that. He glanced over at her. Her lower lip trembled. And, ah, man, she looked ready to cry again. Bryce felt something inside him give, something warm and soft and fuzzy, something that made him want to tell her it'll be all right.

It hit him then.

He liked her. Really, really liked her. Liked-like, as in, I'd-like-to-see-you-again like.

"Thanks, Bryce," she said huskily. "That's probably one of the sweetest things a man's ever said to me."

He shot her a blank stare.

"And you better have meant every word."

She was teasing him, but underneath he could tell she wanted his words to be true. He had the uncontrollable urge to tip her chin up with a gentle hand, an urge he squelched at the last moment, "Ah, yeah. Sure."

She smiled at him, his words obviously having meant a lot to her. "Thanks."

"Don't mention it."

Ah, man. What the *hell* was happening here?

She grew silent. Silence was a good thing, he told himself. Gave him time to think.

"And you can step up the pace a bit if you like," she said.

Yeah. He probably could, but he didn't, too engrossed in his thoughts to want to concentrate on driving. Could he like her, like her? As in seriously like her?

"Wow, we're really moving now."

But the words barely registered. He was attracted to her. He could admit to that, could practically taste those sassy lips of hers.

He turned to look at her, his thoughts as sluggish as the truck, which was why he asked, "Have you ever liked someone so much you were attracted to her?" before he considered the ramification of his words.

She drew back in surprise, and then her expression veiled, the teasing smile left. "What's her name?"

"What's whose name?"

"Never mind. And I've never been attracted to a her, so I really couldn't say."

Well, that answered one question, but not the one he'd wanted. "I mean, attracted to someone because you liked them as opposed to lusted after them."

Another look through lowered lids. "It's Pink Pumps, isn't it?"

"Who?"

She waved her hand. "Never mind, but the answer is, yes, I have."

He was glad he'd asked then. Maybe her answer would give him some insight about what the hell to do about her.

"My college English professor," she added. "In my senior year."

"What'd you do?"

She turned a look on him. "Nothing."

"Nothing?"

She shook her head. "Why bother? Men like my professor never find me attractive, not when they have a whole school of lithe young co-eds to choose from."

"Whoa, whoa, whoa. You're way off the mark with that one," he found himself saying.

"Oh, really? Then why, when I did exactly that—made a

play for a man way out of my league—did he chew me up and spit me out once he was done using me?

"Because he was a fool," Bryce instantly retorted. "Someone who must have been completely blind to what's inside CJ Randall. Believe me, you're better off without a man like that."

He'd rendered her speechless. He could tell. Frankly, he'd rendered himself speechless.

"Thanks," she finally said, but it was in a near whisper.

"You're welcome," he said firmly because, by God, she needed to stop selling herself so short, and he was just the right person to do exactly that.

"And then what'd happened?"

"We didn't talk for the rest of the hour," CJ reported that evening to her fellow workmate-in-bondage, Deanna, trying not to feel even more depressed as she looked around her. The nicotine-colored motel room smelled appropriately like the inside of a cigarette carton. The air conditioner wasn't working. She'd had to beat the darn thing into submission earlier. Now it sputtered and rattled asthmatically beneath the window which she'd left open in the hopes of airing out the place. Unfortunately, it now smelled of grilled onions and frying hamburgers from the burger joint below. It made CJ's stomach growl.

"Not at all?"

CJ sat on the edge of her motel room bed and let her upper body fall back onto the brown spread. "Not a word."

"Well, anybody who says such nice things to you just because you're PMSing should definitely be boinked at the first opportunity."

CJ gasped. "Deanna White, I can't *believe* you said that."

"Why not? I may be married, but I'm not dead."

Trouble was, CJ'd begun to think the same thing. "He's not interested in me, Deanna. He's interested in some anorexic blonde he met yesterday. Not only that, but I couldn't get involved with him even if he did suffer some kind of mental meltdown and find me attractive. Miles would have a fit if I messed around with someone I'm supposed to be interviewing. You know that."

"To hell with Miles."

"Easy for you to say. You're not on his most-wanted list."

"I still think you should go for it."

"There's nothing to go for."

"Since when does the man have to be the aggressor?"

"Forget it, Deanna."

"I'm just saying—"

"No."

"But why not—"

"No."

"You're going to be stubborn about this, aren't you?"

"I am." And she refused to be disappointed by her decision. Refused. Trouble, remember?

Silence, then. "Well, all right." And then, in an obvious change of subject, "So what four-star hotel did Miles book you in tonight?"

"The Bates Motel, where else? You should see it. The carpet looks like termites got desperate one night and chowed down on it, then spit it back out. I think it used to be brown, but I'm not sure. And the bedspread. Ugh. It matches the carpet except for the stains on it. I try not to think about those stains, oh, and the best part is there's a bullet hole in the glass."

"Oh great."

"I doubt I'll get any sleep tonight."

"Score one for Miles."

"Yeah." CJ shot up from the bed again, too agitated to sit down. She pulled a moth-eaten, grunge-brown curtain aside. The view outside wasn't so bad. It offered a scenic vista of the desert sun sinking behind the majestic Burg-O-Rama restaurant sign.

"So how was work today?" CJ tossed back.

"Miles was his usual charming self."

"Oh, yeah?"

"Yeah. Worse than usual, as a matter of fact. I think he misses having you around to publicly flog."

"I wouldn't be surprised."

Deanna's pause was one of long-suffering resignation. "You should have shot him, instead of refusing his advances."

"I wasn't thinking clearly. Remember, he cornered me in the supply closet. I expected him to ask for a ream of copy paper, not ram his you-know-what-into my behind."

"I know what."

"And then I had to go and sock him when he tried to turn me around to kiss me. I have never seen such a look of rage on a man's face before...or so much blood."

"Jeez, Ceej, I wish I could have seen it."

"No you don't. It was terrifying, and demeaning and shocking. I was so stunned I started to cry. I had makeup and tears dripping onto my white rayon blouse. I should have quit then and there. Gone straight to the publisher. Instead I kept my stupid mouth shut because of what happened with Ed and now I doubt anyone would believe me. I blew it and now I'm paying the price. If I could afford to quit, I would, but you know how hard it is to find a job these days. I'm stuck and *he* knows it."

Deanna sighed. "I know. I know. I'm in the same boat." She paused, a depressed sort of pause.

"Speaking of Miles, I better go. I texted the idiot to call this number and I still haven't heard from him. If he calls and the line's busy I'll probably get a lecture about making personal phone calls on the company's dime. You know how it's his mission in life these days to make my life miserable."

"You're probably right."

"I know I'm right."

They rang off, CJ staring at the phone for a long while afterward. When it didn't immediately ring, she breathed a sigh of relief. Gosh, her heart pounded like she'd just run a marathon, the strain on her sore and bruised muscles having increased since she'd sat down. She wanted a shower. Now, before her muscles seized. And she stank. Gracious how she stank...like an Iraqi oil rig. Straightening was an effort too. So was walking.

She took the two small steps required to get from the edge of the bed to the bathroom, turned on the shower, then slowly tugged off her clothes and boots. When she was done, she paused for a moment before the mirror. Deanna was wrong, there was no way Bryce could be interested in her.

She looked like a bag lady.

Her face was streaked with desert dust, the right side burned, the other side not. Her shoulder-length hair looked like she'd taken a wire whisk to it and her bangs stuck straight up exactly like her next door neighbor's yappy dog, Rufus. Terrific. If she wore her "Beam Me Up Scotty" T-shirt she could call

MUFON and pretend she'd been abducted. That'd be a good story.

Now there was an idea. At least she'd get something in print again.

She took a step back instead, studying her body. She told herself it was to see how things were hanging, but she knew better. What she really wanted to see was if it was as bad as she thought. She wanted to observe what Bryce had perused today.

It was bad.

Oh, she wasn't ready for the slaughter house yet, but it was dang close. She turned sideways—no better—then faced forward again. Where the heck had all the weight come from? And why had most of it gone to her breasts? She hadn't noticed it before, but suddenly she admitted that she really did have a decent pair. As yet, they hadn't succumbed to the destructive pull of gravity, and her stomach beneath was relatively flat. It was her hips that would have an African Javaro licking his lips and putting water on to boil. She needed to join a health club...soon...if she could fit through the door, but first she needed to shower.

Fifteen minutes later CJ clicked her hairdryer off and stared at her reflection. Well, at least it didn't stick up straight anymore. And the color matched her sunburn pretty nicely.

"Hello, CJ."

Chapter Six

"Ohmigosh," she screeched, her hand on the handle of the bathroom door and staring at Bryce in disbelief. She glanced down at the towel barely covering her private parts and darted back into the bathroom. "Bryce Danvers, you creep, how the heck did you get in my room?"

"You left your window open. I stuck my hand in and unlocked the door."

She felt her mouth flop open, then closed it, then opened it again. She couldn't believe he was telling the truth, had to resist the urge to call him a liar.

"Well, you can just walk right back out." She clutched the towel around her more firmly, closing the bathroom door until there was just a crack to peek out and hoping upon hope that she was suffering a Dramamine induced hallucination and not facing the reality of Bryce Danvers in her hotel room.

"Ah, honey, you don't really want me to leave, do you?" he drawled in his mint julep voice.

"Don't you call me honey, you...you pervert," she opened the door a bit more. "What's the matter, the woman in pink lose your room number?"

"Who?"

"Never mind. Get out of here before I call security."

"CJ, this place doesn't have security."

"How do you know?"

"'Cause I caught a look at the guy at the front desk. The closest that man had come to security is the maximum security kind."

He must mean that god-awful man at the registration desk, the one with more ink tattooed on his arms than a printing press. "Well, then I'll call the police."

"You'll have to come out here to use the phone."

"That won't be a problem since you're leaving."

"Why? Are you afraid I'm going to bite?"

"I'd need a rabies shot if you did."

He groaned. "Ooo, a low blow."

She didn't say anything. Trouble, she reminded herself.

"And to think, I was going to ask you out to dinner."

"Sorry. I have other plans tonight."

"What plans?"

"None of your business." She heard a rustling sound and stiffened. "Don't you come near me, Bryce Danvers."

Silence.

"Bryce?" she called warily. Maybe he was leaving. She opened the door another notch.

Nothing.

She peeked her head out the door.

"Boo."

She jumped. The brat stood right by the door frame wearing a white polo shirt and tan slacks, looking entirely too good for her peace of mind. "You...You..." She hissed, all the while trying not to gawk. Bryce, without his firesuit, was a sight to behold. The shirt clung to his muscular frame, the white contrasting with his tan and making his eyes stand out even more. She clutched the towel around her more firmly.

"Are those bruises on your shoulder?"

She looked down, startled out of her salivating. Bruises? What bruises?

He walked forward and CJ tensed. Oh gosh, this was bad. This was really, really bad. He smelled like that forest again, and she was in a towel, and he was...oh goodness, he was touching her. Gently, softly touching her shoulder. She closed her eyes, her body thrumming like a guitar string.

"Did the harness give you those?"

She nodded, still not trusting herself to look up at him. If she did, she might drop the towel and offer herself to him like Aphrodite on the altar of love.

"Where else are you bruised?"

"It feels like everywhere I have skin."

"Can I see?"

She looked up at him, there was a look of concern on his face. CJ squelched the stab of disappointment that it wasn't burning, uncontrollable lust.

"C'mon, I promise not to hurt you."

That was what *all* men said, but she lowered the towel anyway, not a lot, just so he could check it out, the feel of his eyes on her more erotic than the feel of his fingers.

"You're black and blue."

Was she? She almost closed her eyes, but the look in his eyes wouldn't allow her. There was so much tenderness in his gaze, so much genuine concern her heart instantly forgave him for not tossing her over his shoulder, throwing her on the bed, and having his wicked way with her.

"Why didn't you tell me the belts hurt you?"

Because she hadn't cared. Because with him sharing the same airspace as her she was hard pressed to notice much of anything. "Because I didn't think it mattered."

His blue eyes narrowed, such pretty blue eyes, so mesmerizing.

"Not matter? Of course it matters."

Oh, gracious, she didn't think she could take much more of being near him. Her body had begun to warm. Places that had no business getting excited suddenly cried out for a little action. And when his finger reached out to touch her again, when she noticed that his eyes had never left her own, the realization that he wanted to kiss her hit her with the force of a club.

"Bryce?" she murmured, unsure, hardly daring to hope that she read his expression correctly.

"Yes," he answered.

But she wasn't mistaken. He *did* want to kiss her. She could tell. Never mind that her common sense demanded a reason as to why he was suddenly interested in her.

Common sense be damned.

"Bryce," she said a second time, and was it her imagination, or did she hear a pleading tone to her voice.

Pleading, definitely pleading, because he'd begun to dip his head. Her ears began to ring.

"Don't get it," he mumbled.

"Don't get what?" she whispered, her eyes on his lips, those wonderful, sensual lips. The ringing grew loud.

Ringing?

It was the phone. Darn, darn, darn. Miles-the-editor-from-Hell. What rotten luck. Or was it? She stiffened, suddenly admitting what she'd been about to do, and with whom. Reality came crashing down. Obviously, pickings were slim out in the desert. Why else would Bryce Danvers, the man who could have absolutely anybody, show up on *her* doorstep?

"CJ—" Bryce begged.

She clutched the towel around her like it was the jacket to her black interview power suit and looked up at him, and for the first time in her life she knew what it meant to get lost in someone's eyes. Never again would she scoff at the silly romantic term. She could feel herself drowning in Bryce, but the jangling of the phone was a persistent reminder of what she was here to accomplish...and it wasn't a night of wild passion.

"I have to get that. It might be my editor." She pulled away.

It *was* Miles, his voice sounding ridiculously cheerful as he said, "Celia, I thought you might have gone out for the evening."

"No, I'm here." The only thing she wished she was out of was her towel, so she clutched the bedspread around her.

Bryce came toward her, and CJ didn't trust the slightly irritated color of his eyes. "Is it him?" he asked.

She gave him a look that said "none of your business".

"Who was that?" Miles asked.

"Hmm? Oh that was the...ah...the TV."

Bryce's eyes narrowed. CJ shot him a look. *Stay back,* her eyes warned, but the irritated look had faded, a devilish one replacing it, a look she'd begun to dread.

"Sounds like you have a man in the room," Miles said suspiciously.

"Miles, if I had Nellis Air Force Base's fifth platoon in here, it would be none of your business."

"Oh, yes it is. Or have you forgotten I have the ability to fire you...for whatever reason?"

He probably would have fired her too, if he wasn't secretly afraid of a sexual harassment lawsuit. That was the only reason she could think of as to why he hadn't done so before now. The shmuck. Whacking off his peepee was too nice. Not that it'd be any great loss. No, his current girl-*fiend* would probably thank her.

"Celia?"

"I'm still here, Miles. And I haven't forgotten."

"Good."

The jerk. The total and utter jerk. But it suddenly it grew hard to concentrate when she noticed Bryce's pants bulged like he'd dropped a fire hose down them.

Jeez, Ceej, talk about lascivious thoughts.

"What was that?" she asked, when it penetrated that Miles had asked her a question.

"I said before you go, how's the article coming?"

She could hear the impatience in his voice, but almost forgot the question all over again when Bryce began to tug off his shirt.

"It's going fine," she choked as Bryce pulled the cotton polo over his head. He had a tan, she noted, with whorls of thick, black hair spreading out from the center of his chest. The shirt dropped to the floor. She turned her head away.

He reached out a hand and gently turned it back toward him. *Look at me,* his eyes said.

"I can't," she answered back.

"Can't? Can't what?"

CJ clutched the phone, beginning to grow frustrated with the whole situation. "I can't...ahh...I can't remember having such a good time."

"The best is yet to come," Bryce whispered.

"Good time?" Miles sounded both disappointed and

disbelieving.

"Yes, Miles, a really good time." Oh, man. This was better than a fantasy. This was every naughty dream she'd ever had all rolled into one. And he wasn't giving up. She almost smiled before she remembered she couldn't get involved with him.

He came toward her, promise in his eyes.

She covered the phone with her hand. "Will you stop it?" she hissed.

In answer he took another step closer. She shoved him back, her hand sinking into his taut stomach with far more force than necessary. He grunted and stepped back.

"What was that?"

"That? It's the TV again. Some action movie."

There was a pause, and when Miles spoke it was with a heavy amount of suspicion. "You know you have a lot riding on this article, Celia."

As if that was news to her. "Thanks for the update, Miles."

"I'd hate to see you fail."

Oh bull, he'd love to see her fail so he could fire her. That was why he'd sent her on this assignment, she suddenly realized. So she could blow it and he could do exactly that.

"Trust me, Miles. I'm on top of things."

She looked up at Bryce, catching the suggestive leer at her words. The man had a mind like a sewer. But he'd stopped unbuttoning those pants of his, thank goodness.

"Fine. I'll want your outline faxed to the office by tomorrow morning."

"Outline? By tomorrow?"

"Is that a problem?"

Not if she wanted to get any sleep tonight. "No, no. I'll fax it first thing."

"And one other thing, Celia."

CJ tensed.

"We expect your behavior to be circumspect while on this assignment."

CJ stiffened. "Are you implying something, Miles?"

A pause. "No. Not at all." She could practically see his smug little smile on his GQ face.

She wanted, oh how she wanted, to tell him that *he* was the one who behaved inappropriately. Instead she hung up on him, glaring up at Bryce, and not adverse to taking out a little of her anger. "What do you think you're doing?"

"Picking up where we left off." He began undoing his pants again.

She shot off the bed, the cover wrapped around her like Cleopatra's cape. *Do not give into temptation, CJ. Do not.* "Stop it, Bryce."

"C'mon, CJ. Don't tell me you can't feel what's happening between us."

She did, but the question was, was it worth getting hurt over? She was not about to become another inductee in the Bryce Danvers' Hall of Shameless Hussies. "Bryce, what I feel for you is—"

"Lust?" he supplied.

"No, I—"

"Uncontrollable passion?"

He was back to plying her with that teasing grin. Damn his parrot blue eyes. Lord help her, some of her anger faded. "No."

"Aroused?"

"Stop it," she said again. How she could have so completely

lost control of the conversation, herself and her brain which suddenly wanted to scream, "Yes! All of the above. Take me I'm yours." Instead, she said, "I won't deny I'm attracted to you."

He gave her that movie star smile that all but jerked the bedspread right off her body.

"But," she hastened to add. "I have a job to do, and getting involved with you is not part of it."

"It could be if you wanted it to be."

And *how* she wanted. "I can't, Bryce."

He took a step toward her. The back of her knees hit the bed.

She held her ground, proudly standing before him, firm in her resolve not to be swayed by his fabulous good looks or that ridiculously sexy smile of his. She was a paragon, a role model for women the world over who were tempted to play with fire.

Who was she kidding?

She wanted him. It was carnal. A basic *me woman, you man* sort of thing. But the reality was, she couldn't have him. Her financial situation was too awful to risk losing her job. And she *would* lose it if word ever got out that she and Bryce had slept together. Miles-the-Editor-from-Hell would make sure of that.

She clutched the bedspread around her and glided as regally as she could to the door. She turned back to him, her hand on the door handle, her meaning obvious.

He was staring at her incredulously, as if he couldn't believe his eyes. "I wouldn't open that door if I were you."

Her hackles rose. "Why not?"

His eyes slid lazily up and down her length, his gaze becoming, if possible, even more heated. "Because you lost your towel back there."

She stared. She'd what? She followed his gaze.

The white towel was by the corner of her bed.

She looked down.

The bedspread had parted to reveal everything from the breast down. She closed her eyes and groaned.

"Not that I'm complaining."

She'd kicked him out. Bryce still couldn't believe it. She'd clutched that bedspread around her, raced forward, grabbed him by the ear and shoved him out the door. He stood outside that door, wishing it would open so he could douse the fire burning through his blood. She'd closed it so hard the brass number six had spun around to become a nine. Damn. He hadn't been this hot for a woman since Gloria Mann in sixth grade. That gave him pause for a second, a pause which he ignored. He liked getting her goat. And she was cute. And tired. And *bruised*.

He frowned.

Maybe he shouldn't have made her ride along for the day. She'd looked about ready to drop. He caught a whiff of Burg-O-Rama, an idea coming to mind. He'd get her something to eat. Sort of a peace offering, since it was obvious that was all he was getting tonight. But he could wait. He was a patient man. Once he decided on something, he wouldn't give up until he had it.

And he wanted CJ.

Half an hour later he stood before her door again, the sound of tapping on a keyboard came through the open window. The smell of a Burg-O-Rama special wafted up from the red and white bag he carried in one hand. He held a soda in the other, using his knuckles to knock on the door. When she opened it, he was surprised at the burst of tenderness he felt.

Must be the oversized T-shirt, he thought. She looked adorable. Like a little kid playing dress up. Unfortunately, the look in her eyes was one-hundred-percent adult. She looked ready to kick him in the you-know-whats.

He quickly held up the bag, saying, "Peace offering," before she could slam the door in his face.

The door stopped mid-swing. "What is it?" she asked suspiciously.

"Smell."

She sniffed experimentally, her expression touchingly full of hunger. "Food," she breathed almost reverently.

"A hamburger, Coke and French fries...at least I think they're fries. They were a little worse for wear when I looked at them. So I ate a few." He smiled winningly. "Am I forgiven?"

"No. But I'll take the food."

He laughed, couldn't seem to stop himself. "Here, take it."

She reached out and grabbed the bag, hugging it to her like it was the Last Supper.

"You got dressed," he noted, trying not to laugh at the white T-shirt with *Save a whale...feed me food* on the front. It hung down to her knees.

"Yeah, well, the bedspread didn't match my towel."

"Too bad," he said. "Oh. I also bought you this." He reached into his back pocket and held up a tube of Aspri-gel. "Muscle cream. Guaranteed to cure what ails ya. I was tempted to buy a tube of Harry's Easy-In lubricant, but I thought that might be pushing matters. No pun intended."

"Very funny." She reached for the box.

"Ahh, ahh, ahh." He held it above his head. "Don't I get to rub it on?"

"No."

"Then how 'bout a kiss?"

She frowned. "Dream on."

He took a step forward and kissed her on the lips anyway. The smell of greasy burgers drifted between them.

"Sneak," she grumbled, but Bryce was delighted by the fact that she didn't seem too upset. She'd opened the door when she'd seen him outside which, given the window's proximity to the front door, she must have spotted him. And she hadn't slammed the door in his face once he'd kissed her.

"Sure you don't want me to buy that Easy-In lubricant?"

"Positive. But feel free to buy it for yourself. I'm sure your hand will thank you."

He laughed, not even minding when she smiled at him victoriously, just before slamming the door in his face...at last.

Chapter Seven

"Gosh, what am I going to do?" CJ asked Deanna later that night. It was nearing midnight—eleven thirty to be exact—but Deanna's night appeared to be just getting started. She'd called her on the way to a club. "What do I say to the man when I see him?" She asking, pacing from one end of the hotel room to the next. She pitched her voice low. "Gee, Bryce, thanks for almost boinking me, but I really feel going to bed with you would be a mistake."

"That would work," Deanna agreed. It sound like she had the window down, or she was calling her from inside a vacuum cleaner. Deanna's hands free unit always sounded that way.

"No, it *wouldn't* work, Deanna. Miles would throw a fit."

"Screw Miles."

"No thanks. I had a chance to do that once before but the idea still fills me with revulsion."

"Then screw Bryce."

"Deanna!"

"Well, why not?"

"Because I have bills to pay, a car payment, I'm two months behind on rent, and if I miss another payment I'll be evicted. I can't afford to risk losing my job. Jeesh, if only that position I interviewed for would call, but until then, I can't."

"What if—"

"On the other hand," CJ went on, "if Miles never finds out, what can it hurt?"

"Nothing, but—"

"So I should do it, right? That's what you're saying."

"I think—"

"Damn I wish he hadn't kissed me," CJ muttered, pacing the three steps in the other direction. "Now I can't get him out of my mind. And afterward, he'd been all set to strip and play bedroom aerobics, and I'd actually been willing to play aerobics instructor. But there's nothing wrong with that, is there, Deanna? I mean, I haven't been involved with a man since the turn of the century. Well, maybe not that long. But it feels that long. So if he wants to take it all the way, I should let him, right?"

There was a long silence on the phone. CJ waited for Deanna to speak. She didn't.

"Deanna...are you there?"

"I'm just waiting to see if you're finished."

CJ paused in her pacing. "Sorry. What do you think?"

Deanna sighed. "CJ, you know what my advice to you has been from the very beginning."

"Go for it."

"That's right."

CJ shook her head. "The thing is, I checked out my body last night. It's not a pretty sight. I didn't think it was possible for a woman's butt to spread so much."

"Wait till you're thirty."

"I'm serious, Deanna. People are going to start stamping wide load on the back of my pants."

Deanna snorted.

"And I can't fit into any of my jeans. I'm down to one pair, the ones I'm wearing now."

"Join the club."

"I'm starting to think I should wire my jaw shut."

"You're not fat," Deanna said, chuckling.

"I feel like it." She plopped down on the bed.

"Besides, the man's already seen you naked."

"He's seen me in a towel."

"For part of the time, anyway."

"Thanks for reminding me."

"My pleasure."

CJ released a sigh. "What if I take off my clothes and he runs out of the room?"

"You could always wear a paper bag."

"That'd only cover my head. It's my body, especially my backside I want to hide."

"CJ—"

"You could feed a family for a year with the fat on my thighs."

"Look, you like the man, right?"

CJ looked down into her jean-clad lap before whispering the word, "Yes." Even if he was Trouble incarnate. But the truth was, he'd melted her resistance yesterday with his kind words, concerned manner and teasing blue eyes. And that kiss.

"Then trust your instincts."

"But what if I get hurt?" Again, she silently added.

"How can you get hurt when all you want is a one night stand?"

"You're right. A one-night stand. That's all I want. All I need."

"Gee, Bryce, I'd really like to screw your brains out," CJ practiced as she walked through the crowded staging area the next morning. No, that didn't sound right. "Howdy, sailor, can I buy you a drink?"

"Sure," said the baseball capped man walking by.

CJ blushed to the tips of her sunburned ear. "Er, ahh, not you."

She ducked her head and kept on walking.

With each step she took she became more and more nervous. She'd dreamed about Bryce all night. Sultry, erotic dreams where he'd kissed her senseless and made her moan with pleasure. She'd woken knowing there was no sense in fighting it. He was an itch that needed to be scratched and so what was wrong with indulging herself?

You're not that kind of girl.

True. But there was no reason why she couldn't be. At least once in her life.

There were hundreds of people out, the smell of exhaust mixing with the dust. The nearest town was about thirty miles away and the only thing she could see in the distance was cactus, cactus and, oh yeah, more cactus. Still, that didn't stop people from crowding between the big rigs that carted the race trucks from staging area to staging area. She'd bet every person within a two hundred mile radius drove in every day, well, with the exception of the kids from Harmony Haven. She'd gotten digital copies of some photos of Bryce with the kids and CJ hadn't been able to stop herself from perusing them once or twice.

He was such a nice man. Too bad he was Trouble.

Unfortunately, finding that Trouble amidst the crowd was like trying to find pantyhose in an auto parts store. And every time one of the crew members used an air-ratchet she just about jumped out of her skin.

She did manage to find the Star Oil transporter parked in a long line of big rigs and tried to distract herself from her fears by studying the haulers. The vehicles were amazing pieces of equipment. The top quarter was dedicated to storing spare parts, a separate hauler used to tote the race trucks from staging area to staging area. The bottom two-thirds of the vehicle was a mini-workshop, with a long aisle stretching down the center with floor-to-ceiling white (and wasn't it just like a man to pick that grease-enhancing color?) cabinets lining either side. At the end was a lounge complete with TV, VCR, couch and other man-type necessities.

With a nod at the crew, each of whom smiled that we-got-you-good smile, she headed down the main isle of the hauler and the lounge, her palms sweaty with anticipation.

But the moment she opened the door, she knew she'd made a mistake. The mirrored walls gave her a three dimensional view of Bryce embracing a lanky brunette, her arms wrapped around his waist like an octopus hugging its prey.

"Oh, excuse me," CJ said, before she hastily stepped back out the door, but not before Bryce looked up.

"CJ, wait."

Wait? Hah! Like she'd wait for him. She'd sooner wait for the plague. What a fool she'd been. The man obviously couldn't keep his zipper up for more than five seconds. She hoped he choked on a bottle of Easy-In. Hoped a condom cut off his blood supply so Little Bryce atrophied.

"CJ." She could hear him running to catch up to her, but the long aisle seemed to have stretched an additional twenty feet. His hand touched her arm. She jerked away. Furious beyond belief.

"CJ, c'mon. You're acting like a jealous lover."

She stopped, sprang back to face him and blasted him with a glare. "I am *not* your lover."

"No, but you could be if you wanted to." He gave her a leer.

She placed her hands on her hips. "You disgust me."

He gave her that boyish look of hurt that she'd begun to hate. It seemed to say, "I was just playin' around."

Not with her. No way.

He lurched past her and placed a hand on her shoulder when she tried to dart past him. "CJ, wait. Seriously, that wasn't what it looked like."

"Oh, really. Were you just sniffing her hair?"

She heard someone choke and glanced behind him. The brunette stood there. Tall. Elegant. Beautiful. CJ hated her on sight, not very nice, but there it was.

"No, I was not. Here. Let me introduce you."

Introduce her? To the latest notch in his bedpost? Over her size ten, water-retaining body. Man, she couldn't believe she'd actually contemplated becoming one of those notches.

He turned toward the woman. "This is Kathleen...a good friend."

A good friend? Yeah right. She was probably good all right. In bed. She shot the woman a glare, then looked back at Bryce. "You're sick."

The woman choked again. For the first time she took a good look at her, and noticed the tears smearing her once perfectly applied makeup. Her brows rose. Bryce was a good kisser, but to move a woman to tears?

"Hi," the brunette said, holding out her hand, her misty smile warm and friendly.

CJ would rather shake hands with a leper.

"Kathleen is Nick Seaver's wife."

Nick Seaver, racing legend, one of the "Pros" referred to in the Pro/Am part of race.

The woman's hand dropped back to her side, eyes full of concern. "Bryce's told me so much about you, CJ."

He had? Told her what? That she had nice breasts like he told everybody else?

"Perhaps we could all have dinner together one night soon?" She wiped a tear off her cheek, before turning back to Bryce. Her expression softened. "I don't know how to thank you—"

Bryce held up his hands, interrupting her flow of words. "Don't thank me, Kathleen. It's no big deal."

"Yes, it is—"

"No, it's not. Nick would do the same for me if he were in my position. Besides, I owe him something for taking the time to teach me how to drive Big Foot out there."

CJ rolled her eyes and snorted. Apparently, he wasn't a very good teacher. "That's not saying much."

Kathleen gave her a look of surprise before turning back to Bryce. Her enormous lavender eyes misted again. "You're a good friend."

CJ looked between the two, suddenly realizing Bryce must be telling the truth. There was no way a woman could fake the look of gratitude on Kathleen's face. Her anger faded as her journalistic sense kicked in, but she refused to let Bryce see how much she was dying to know what was going on.

Cool. Professional. In control, she reminded herself.

But it was hard to contain her rampant curiosity when Kathleen was looking up at Bryce as if he were the Patron Saint of Selflessness. The woman turned to look at her, her expression one of kindness. "You've got a good man, here, CJ. I'd hold on to him if I were you."

The only thing she wanted to hold onto was his Little Bryce, but she couldn't tell the other woman that.

"If there's anything I can ever do for you…"

Like what? Loan me your push up bra, CJ thought. It wouldn't fit.

With one last watery, and to CJ's mind, melodramatic smile, Kathleen turned away, leaving the transporter in a trail of Passion.

CJ swung back to Bryce, unable to resist one little dig, just one. "What'd you do? Donate sperm so she could have a child?"

He chuckled, crossing his arms over his ivory-colored polo, a shirt that CJ couldn't help but notice clung to his body like wax. He'd also left the two buttons open, almost as if he knew how badly she wanted to run her fingers through the hair on his chest.

"CJ, your comments never cease to amuse me."

"Yeah, well, maybe I should chuck it all and start a sitcom."

He laughed again before saying, "I promised Nick Seavers I'd sponsor their race team next year."

"You're sponsoring a truck next year, Bryce?"

CJ glanced at the entrance. Harry stood there, his bushy gray brows arched, the white team outfit with a red star on the front making him look like the Pillsbury Doughboy with a target tattooed to his chest.

"Yeah."

CJ returned her gaze to Bryce. "That's it?" she asked in amazement. "Kathleen Seavers acted like she was naming her first born after you all because you agreed to sponsor a silly race truck?"

"Watch it," Harry snapped.

Bryce looked past her. "She doesn't mean anything by that, Harry."

"Yeah, well, maybe she don't know how much money you just agreed to drop."

"I haven't dropped it yet."

"Yeah, but you will. You're a man of your word, Bryce."

"Well, thank you, Harry."

CJ all but rolled her eyes. Jeesh, they sounded like politicians. "How much does sponsoring a race truck cost? A couple thousand?"

Harry stared down at her incredulously before throwing back his head and roaring with laughter. He had three gold teeth, CJ noted disgruntledly, and they needed a darn good cleaning. "Well, so then how much does it cost?"

"Try a couple *million*," Harry provided gleefully.

"*Million?*" She gaped. "Jeez, no wonder she was looking at you like she wanted to have your baby. *I'd* have your baby for a couple million dollars."

"You would?"

CJ's cheeks flamed with color. Bryce must have noticed because his smile widened.

"Shoot, Bryce," Harry said. "If I'd known you were in the market to sponsor a truck I would've asked you to sponsor one of mine."

Bryce finally broke eye contact, CJ feeling like a puppet whose string had been cut loose when he looked away. "It wasn't something I'd planned on doing."

Harry took a pull of his cigar. "Yeah, well, I suppose Nick needs it more than I do. He was going to lose his team if you hadn't agreed to do it."

"I know," Bryce said.

CJ stared at him in amazement. That he would do that for a friend amazed her. She didn't know why, it just did. It was as if she'd suddenly discovered an old oil painting in her attic that turned out to be worth a mint. Man, if he were any other man she'd be all over him like baby oil. She wouldn't want just a one night with him. She'd want...

Uh oh.

She refused to go down *that* road. She stared up at him, his eyes having never left her own. Her body revved in response, just heated up like a motor at a starting line.

Escaaaape, screamed her mind.

"Hey, where're you going?" he drawled.

She didn't know, she just knew if she didn't leave she'd do something really stupid...like stroke the side of his jaw and tell him what a nice guy he was. "To the bathroom," she said instead. She squeezed past Harry, who stared down at her speculatively. The man smelled like an exhaust pipe.

"Hang on. I'll go with you."

That was the last thing she needed. "I can *go* by myself, thank you." She stepped out into the morning sunshine; the desert air sucked the moisture right out of her face. She'd have crow's feet by the end of the race.

"Are you sure? I can pull your pants down for you if you want."

She stopped and turned to face him. "No thanks. The only person who gets to see me without *my* pants is my doctor."

Although a half-hour ago she'd been of a different mind. Now she wasn't so certain even a one-night stand was a good idea.

He wagged his eyebrows at her. "Lucky doctor."

And he *was* lucky, Bryce thought, watching her huff away. Wow, the woman had a walk that could catch the eyes of a blind man.

"You like her."

Bryce never took his eyes off her. "Yeah, I do."

"She's not your usual type," Harry said.

"So you've said before."

"But you still like her."

"I do."

"You gonna make her ride along with you all day today?"

"No," Bryce said. "She's got bruises all over her body."

"Does she now?"

Bryce glanced over at Harry. "It's not what you think."

"No?"

"Not yet at least," Bryce added.

"You're on your way to saying I do, if you don't watch it."

Bryce turned toward his friend. "Don't be ridiculous, Harry. I just met her."

"So? When's that ever stopped a woman from dragging a man to the altar? Fact is, you're what them dames call 'a catch'. What makes you think she's not after your money? Like Lana."

Ooo. Low blow, but one that was to be expected. Harry was his best friend, one who had his best interest at heart. "She's nothing like Lana." And she wasn't. Lana had been like those vacation packages you're sometimes offered: too good to be true.

"How do you know?"

"Because, Harry, if she was after my money, she wouldn't have tossed me outta her hotel room last night."

One of Harry's bushy brows rose. "So. She's smarter than the rest. It's called baiting the hook."

Bryce shook his head in exasperation. "And if she was like Lana, why does she wear those baggy jeans and big T-shirts."

"To get your interest up."

"No, you're wrong. She not after me. I can tell. Why, she actually takes pleasure in insulting me." He smiled, recalling some of her better barbs. "She's just fighting the attraction. I get the feeling she doesn't trust me or something."

"Would you trust you?"

He stared at his friend a long moment. "Good question."

Harry shrugged. "I dunno. Maybe there *is* something between the two'a you. I certainly can't recall you ever going after a woman who looks like her."

"What do you mean, a woman who looks like her?" Bryce asked, instantly irritated.

"You know. Not glitzy. Kind of a dog."

"She's *not* a dog."

Harry's brows rose.

"She's gorgeous." He turned back to watch her. "Just look at her. Those eyes. As green as fish tank rock. And her figure. Like ripe melons." He outlined the shape of a woman with his hands. "And I just know she's going to be something in bed. CJ's the type of person who probably keeps it bottled up all day, then wham, catches you by surprise at night. Add in her spunky personality and she's darn near perfect." He turned back to his friend.

"Oh, yeah?"

"Yeah."

Harry didn't say anything for a long moment. Trucks roared off in the distance, the crew moved around them, each man listening, no doubt, to their conversation.

"You've got it bad, bud," he said at last. "You've got it *real* bad."

Nah. Harry had it all wrong. He just really liked CJ. And Harry was blind if he didn't see her beauty. His friend needed to look beneath the freckles to the women beneath. That was the woman Bryce'd gotten a glimpse of last night, the woman he found so damn attractive, despite the bruises. He'd *hated* seeing those bruises. She didn't deserve bruises; she deserved champagne and caviar and warm, candle-lit baths. It was something he had a feeling she'd never had.

But she *would* have it. Hell, he'd take her to his home in Aspen and show her how to take a real bath. He'd use the one in his master bedroom, the one with windows overlooking the mountains. Maybe light some candles. He'd heard women like candles, especially the smelly ones. Yeah. He got hard just thinking of it.

He watched as CJ disappeared around the corner of a big rig. Now, if he could just convince her to come to Aspen with him.

One step at a time, Bryce. One step at a time.

A half hour later CJ entered the lounge after first making sure it wasn't occupied. A blast of cool air hit her as she entered. Ahh. Air conditioning. After twenty-five minutes of wandering around in the heat, it felt like heaven. Leave it to a man to put air conditioning in a rolling garage, she thought, sitting down on the black leather couch taking up two walls of the room. Frankly, she was surprised there wasn't a La-Z-Boy in here too.

She leaned back, studying a drawing Daniel had made for them, the child's squiggly signature in the bottom right corner. It said "Go Bryce" in thick, blue crayon, a wobbly edged drawing of a truck beneath it. Cute. Too bad it reminded her of a man she was trying very hard to forget. She leaned back and closed her eyes, inhaling deeply and imagining she could smell that yummy Bryce smell.

Tangy. Masculine Bryce. Hot, steamy Bryce. She tingled all over just thinking about him, and she'd been thinking about him a lot, not just because of the Nick Seavers thing, no that had only made it worse. How could you dislike a man who bought toys for little kids and bailed a friend out of trouble? You couldn't. So now on top of being one sexy man, he was also one damn nice man. Plus there was the added problem of the little twinge her heart had given when she'd caught him in Kathleen's arms.

She could handle lust for Bryce, no problem. She could *not*, under any circumstances, handle involvement. And that little twinge had proven to her that she was starting to like Bryce just a little too much. So that was that. No one night stand. From here on out she would act mature, in control of the situation, and *not*, under any circumstance, get involved with the man. *He* didn't need to know every time he came near her she just about wet her pants.

"There you are."

She just about really *did* wet her pants. Jeesh, what'd he have, stealth shoes or something? She looked up at him and pasted an over-large smile on her face. "Oh, Bryce. Hi."

He smiled back, his eyes sweeping her up and down as he reclined against the door frame. "I've been looking everywhere for you."

"You have? Really? Gee, and I've been here the whole time."

He looked at her funny.

She clenched her hands in her lap and refused to move. "Was there something you wanted?"

Dumb, dumb, dumb thing to say, CJ. His eyes narrowed, the look in them grew heated. He entered the lounge, the door closing softly behind him. "Oh, yeah, I want something all right."

Her cheeks stung with color. "Something you wanted to talk to me about," she gritted out.

"Yeah. A couple of things. I think you should ride along for an hour today. You're too bruised to do much more than that."

She wanted to hug him. She really did. Sure, Miles might pitch a fit, but she didn't care. She just didn't care."

"No problem," she said. "What was the other thing?"

"I want to get together with you tonight."

Her eyes narrowed.

"For dinner," he quickly added.

Yeah, right, a little wine, a little soft music and *blam*, he'd be on top of her. But she'd changed her mind about the odds of that ever happening and so she said, "Gee, Bryce, I'm really sorry, but I have other plans."

He stared down at her for a long time, the look on his face growing puzzled. "CJ, what's wrong? You haven't insulted me once since I've come in here."

"I haven't? Gee, I'll have to work on that."

"And you're looking at me funny too."

"I am?"

"Yeah, like I'm an ex-boyfriend you just met on the street or something." He sat down next to her. She didn't move, even though every instinct was telling her to get out of Dodge, *fast*, but she'd done that once only to land in the same situation again.

"Are you feeling okay?"

"Fine."

"Your bruises hurting?"

"No."

"Then you're not still mad at me, are you?"

Her heart pinged in her chest like gravel on the underside of the truck. "Mad, why would I be mad?"

He shifted in his seat, sliding closer to her. "For breaking into your room last night." His voice grew lower, his eyes fixed on her lips.

"No. Why would that bother me? I tossed you out on your ear. Literally."

"You did, didn't you?" he said softly, placing his hand on her thigh.

She just about leapt off the couch.

"But then you opened the door to me again and so I figured you couldn't be *that* mad."

She was in trouble, deep, deep doo-doo. Just his touch set her heart racing, just the feel of his fingers, gentle, yet with an underlying edge of hardness, had the ability to make her admit something; she was losing control of her willpower.

"CJ?'

Man, she was sick of this. She was sick of always being a good girl. Of resisting one-night stands. She was sick of how he could reduce her to a quivering mass of Jell-O by just by saying her name. The ivory polo he wore enhanced the blueness of his eyes, turning them a color reminiscent of peacock feathers. He had such beautiful eyes.

"Bryce, don't."

He was leaning toward her. "Don't what?"

"Do what you're about to do."

"And what's that?" His breath drifted across her face. He'd been sucking on a breath mint, she could tell.

She started to breathe hard. Oh, man. There it was again. That smell. Tangy. Masculine. Bryce.

"You're going to kiss me." But the words came out sounding like an order.

His eyes narrowed. The look in them intensified, almost as if he knew every naughty thought, every nasty idea she had floating in the hormonal cauldron of her mind. Every nerve suddenly went on red alert. Heat shimmered through her body. *Run, CJ. Run away now.*

"Oh, sweetheart, I am *definitely* going to kiss you."

Chapter Eight

Of course she wasn't going to run. Who was she trying to kid? Instead, she retreated a couple inches.

He scooted closer to her. She retreated again.

"Why are you fighting this?" he groaned, his voice a husky timbre that sent mating hormones into overdrive. Not good. Not good at all.

"Fighting this?" she scoffed. "Who's fighting anything? I, ahh, I just have an itch on my bu— Ahh, my back." She demonstrated by rubbing her shoulders back and forth against the black leather couch, trying not to wince when her sore muscles twinged.

"I have an itch too…for you." And she could see the truth in his eyes. It made her heart want to sing "I Feel Pretty" or something, because when he looked at her like that, she really *did* feel pretty. Beautiful, even.

"God, you're something," he said softly, as if reading her mind.

She was not "something". She was a nothing. The type of woman men liked to make a pass at, but nothing more. An easy mark. Someone so desperate for attention she'd settle for anything—or so those men had thought, but then she forgot everything as he leaned forward.

She should have pulled away. She tried to tell herself that, but Self wouldn't listen.

"I'm going to kiss you," he said.

Yes, please.

She was dreaming again. Bryce couldn't really be staring down at her like she was the oil in his motor. He moved his head toward her as if he had every intention of placing those wonderful, sensual lips against hers. Her body stretched taut...waiting. His breath wafted across her face. She closed her eyes.

Soft. His lips were so soft. They were merely nudging hers, seeking, asking that she open to him. His hand touched her shoulder softly, then instantly moved away as if he remembered her bruises, only to move up to stroke her jaw. Then she was kissing him back, giving vent to every wild fantasy she'd had about him. Her mouth opened, his taste flooded her; minty and sweet. A gentle brush of his tongue and her body coiled like a spring.

He deepened the kiss; she answered his need by tilting her head, giving him all she had to offer, and more. His hand released her chin, traveling down the side of her neck, searing a trail of heat down her collarbone, hovering just for a moment above her breast. *Yes,* her body said. *Oh yes.*

She arched into him wanting him to suckle her, to, good gracious, to bite her, but instead his hands skimmed over her arms, then pulled her closer to him. She moaned in disappointment. He didn't seem to notice.

And the kiss went on.

She lost herself in it, existing in a place somewhere between reality and hot desire. She could feel him hard against her leg. She rubbed into him, knowing it was wanton, uncaring that it was. Her ears began to ring, her heart pounded.

She moaned, wanting his mouth on her too.

The shirt she wore slipped out of her waistband like tissue from a box. Cool air from the AC raised goose pimples on her flesh. She leaned back and lay on the couch; Bryce followed her down. His hand touched her stomach and her skin contracted. His fingers worked on the buttons of her jeans. His mouth continued its sensuous assault, his other hand raising her shirt higher. And higher. She helped him by tugging on it too, the blood rushing through her ears as she waited for the feel of his lips against her breast.

With a savvy that bespoke years of practice, Bryce undid the catch in the front of her bra. It twanged open with a snap. CJ opened her eyes, catching Bryce's hot, intense glare just before his lips captured her nipple.

Maybe it was because she hadn't been with a man since Prohibition, or maybe it was because she turned into a sex-crazed maniac around Bryce, but the sight of him working that nipple, playing with it, teasing it, just about sent her to climax heaven. His lips were cool against her sizzling flesh; his teeth nipped her, made the ache between her legs throb.

His other hand crept in the open vee of her jeans. She wished she wasn't wearing panties. She wanted them gone, wanted to feel Bryce's hand brush against her curls...wanted his finger to trace up her wet, hot valley...wanted whoever it was to stop knocking on the dang door.

"Go away," Bryce ordered.

"Bryce?"

It was Harry.

CJ jumped, then hastily pulled down her shirt, nearly clocking Bryce on the nose in the process.

"What do you want, Harry?" Bryce asked, his hand still exploring the inside of her jeans.

"Stop it," she hissed, trying to pull his hand out, hoping, praying Harry didn't get it in his head to open the door, not that he wouldn't know what they'd been doing anyway. Her lips felt as big as sturgeon's and her nipple felt like it'd done battle with a Hoover vacuum and lost.

"Is CJ in there with you?"

"I'm right here, Harry." She leveled Bryce with a glare. "Would you get your hand out of my pants, please?"

"It's stuck," he said with that bad-boy smile.

"Are you two kids coming?" Harry asked.

"I was just about to," Bryce told her.

CJ ignored him. *Coming?* What did Harry mean, coming? She glanced at her watch. "Holy moly," she gasped. "Bryce, we've got to be at the starting line in five minutes."

"I know."

"You know?"

"That's what I came in here to tell you."

"Oh, great!" She grabbed his wrist and jerked his hand out from between her thighs, then pushed on his shoulders, forcing him to sit back up. He looked disappointed. "I haven't even gotten into my firesuit."

"I'd rather see you in your birthday suit."

She'd rather see him in his too, but one of them had to be sensible.

Five minutes later the truck roared to life, fans around the starting line watching them intently, not that CJ noticed. Her hands shook as she double-checked her harness because she honestly couldn't remember buckling it. Man, what had just happened? She felt as brainless as a blonde. Well, maybe not *that* brainless.

"Ready?"

No, but she nodded anyway. The desert sun was already high above them, sending waves of heat up from the road. It would be another day from hell. The damn seatbelts would dig into her shoulders for hours. Terrific.

"Do you have your harness on correctly?"

"I think so."

"Maybe you ought to check it one more time."

She looked down at the same time he did, though Bryce roared with laughter while she shrieked at the...the *thing* rising up like a serpent from her safety belt. A plastic penis.

"Omigosh, how did that get there?"

They had glued it to her lap belt, she realized. When she'd pulled the racing harness taut, the plastic *thing* had lifted to attention. Those jerks.

"It's Kong Dong."

She didn't care what it was, just as long as it was gone, unfortunately, it was impossible to remove. She tugged on it as hard as she could, but it wouldn't budge.

Bryce laughed harder.

CJ wasn't laughing. With each successive tug she grew more and more irate. "It...won't...budge," she muttered through clenched teeth as she pulled with all her might.

"That because it's plastic."

She wanted to hit him, she really did. "Tell Kevin to get it out of here."

"I can't."

"Why not?"

"Because we're leaving."

"We're what—" Her words died in her throat as she was

109

thrown back into her seat, the motor roaring in her ears as Bryce gunned the engine with her hands still clutched around the Kong Dong like a joy stick. The force of their departure ripped it away from the belt. CJ held it before her victoriously, her hand bouncing up and down with the motion of the truck. The thing looked real. She chastised herself for even noting that much. She shoved it between the net and the window sill, darting a look backward just in time to see fans rush forward to see what it was she'd tossed. A smile, her first one in hours, spread across her face as she envisioned their reactions.

"You didn't want to keep it?"

The people dotting the road were reduced to blobs of color as they picked up speed. CJ faced forward again, smile fading. "No."

"Probably just as well. You've already got more than a handful right here." He wiggled in his seat.

The truck lurched over a bump, CJ rolled her eyes. "Don't start with the sexual innuendoes, Bryce. I'm not in the mood."

His smile faded. He nodded. "Yeah, you're probably right. We need to talk about what just happened."

CJ released a frustrated breath. "I don't want to talk about it. I lost control for a second or two, that was all."

"That's not all, CJ, and you know it. There's something happening between us."

She crossed her arms in front of her. "Yeah, something that will end the minute this race is over."

He shot her a wounded look. "What's that supposed to mean?"

"I'm not your type."

"Yes ,you are."

"Yeah, you're probably right. Everybody with a pulse is

your type," she reasoned. "I tried to tell you this earlier but you, ah, sidetracked me in the transporter."

"Look, CJ. You *are* my type. Why else would I show up at your motel last night?"

"Because you lost Pink Pumps's phone number."

He shot her an irritated look. "Just who the hell is this Pink Pumps you keep referring to?"

He sounded so frustrated, and so utterly at his wit's end, she said, "The one with a size four waist and breast implants. You know, the woman you met the day before the race started."

"Who..." And then his head slowly tipped back before he nodded. "You mean Michelle."

"Is that her name? I thought it'd be Lola or Babette or something."

He ignored her sarcasm. "CJ, I'm not interested in her."

"Oh yeah? Then what was all that stuff yesterday about liking someone so much you're attracted to them, although what's not to like about that woman is hard to understand?"

He glanced over at her, his eyes suddenly intent. "CJ, I was talking about *you*."

Words failed her for a long, long second, a second in which two bugs committed insecticide on the front windshield and a little squirrel darted halfway across the road, saw the truck racing toward it, then darted back. Smart squirrel. She swallowed back her pleasure and said, "Oh, yeah?"

"Yeah."

Ah, man. That was twice in two days he'd said something that took her breath away. Sheesh, her heart couldn't take much more of this. Never mind that it was sorta a backhanded compliment. Obviously, he wasn't attracted to her looks, which might actually be a compliment. Man. She didn't know what to think. But she was still inordinately pleased, right before her sense of logic chose that moment to rear its unwanted head. *Trouble, remember?*

Yeah, but she was starting to like Trouble.

Enough to risk a broken heart? her mind immediately retorted. *Sure, he's being nice to you now, but you just know once the race is over he'll go back to his usual fare. You're a novelty right now.*

Gee, thanks, Mind.

But Mind was right, she just hadn't wanted to admit it at first. If nothing else, her research had revealed Bryce's short attention span where the fairer sex was concerned.

"Look, Bryce, you've been really nice, but I—" She jerked in her seat suddenly, the belts causing her to gasp. "Look out," she screamed. But Bryce had already seen it, was just then slamming on the brakes to avoid the curve in the road.

The harness dug into her shoulders like her bra on a heavy bloat day. CJ almost lost her breakfast on Bryce's asbestos tennis shoes it hurt so bad. They slid, screeched and spun around a bend. Her butt puckered so hard it almost stuck to the seat. She closed her eyes, praying God would take pity on her, not that she'd been listening lately. Only when the truck straightened out again did she reluctantly, and very slowly, open her eyes. They were still upright. Amazing.

"Waah whoooo," Bryce cried, shifting in his seat like a kid on Christmas day. "Man, that was *great*. I'm gonna have to get us one of these things."

Us, she thought. "Great?" she said instead. "Great? You call instant hemorrhoids fun? You call more bruises fun? You call almost losing my breakfast fun? I don't think so."

"Hey. It's not my fault," he said laughingly. "I was so busy staring at the outline of your breasts I forgot to look ahead."

Oh great. She was surprised she hadn't screamed in horror. She shifted in her seat, then reached down to adjust the harness in her lap.

He looked over at her, and she could hear the leer in his southern drawl. "Need some help?"

"What I *need* is for you to keep your dang eyes on the road."

"I'd rather keep them on you."

"I don't want them on me. Don't you get it? I was about to tell you we're through."

"Through? We haven't even begun."

"You know what I mean. It's over."

"But we've barely started."

"Would you *stop* it?

"Who's on first?"

"Be serious!"

"I am Serious and you're Chicken, What's on third."

"I am not Chicken. And I don't want to get involved with you, so there."

The truck leapt over a bump. CJ braced herself as they landed, a hiss escaping her lips as the nylon straps dug into her once more.

His eyes smiled at her, the look in them openly teasing. "Has Harry been telling horror stories about me again?" he drawled in his cute Southern accent.

She gritted her teeth and clipped out, "No."

"Good. I hate it when he does that."

That did it. She had officially reached her breaking point. "The reason I don't want to get involved with you is because I'm sleeping with my editor."

"The one who thinks you're sleeping with the 5th platoon?"

Man, she was going to strangle him. "All right, so maybe we're not really lovers, but he wanted to be lovers. I turned him down. Ever since then he's been looking for an excuse to fire me."

"So? Quit."

"He told me if I quit he'd spread a rumor that I was plagiarizing stories...to be specific, *his* stories. So I've been sticking it out. Saying the word plagiarize in the journalism industry is like yelling fire in a crowded theater."

"He sounds like a real putz. All the more reason to quit."

CJ almost screamed. "It took me two years to find that job," she snapped. "Two years of doing temp work, of living hand to mouth, of putting up with one rotten employer after another. Two years," she yelled, "and two weeks after I start at *DRIVE*, two weeks to the day, Miles makes a pass at me. He's never forgiven me for punching him out, and he never will. I know that.

"Just as I know that if I mess up on this assignment, make one wrong move—believe me, getting involved with you would be a *big* wrong move in *his* book—then I'm out, and you can bet your you-know-what I'll never find another job in journalism."

"So?"

She gave up. The man was impossible. It was hopeless. She leaned back in her seat, crossed her arms over her chest and stared out the side window in silence. She hoped he asphyxiated on exhaust fumes.

"Hey. Does this mean we can't get together tonight?"

She glared over at him and for the first time in her life felt the nearly uncontrollable urge to reach out, grab a man by the testicles and squeeze.

Hard.

Really hard.

"Because I have to tell you I'm coming to your hotel room tonight anyway."

For the first time that morning Bryce Danvers sounded absolutely serious. Funny thing was, instead of scaring the hell out of her, it sent a fission of electricity through her obviously sex-starved body.

"Well, then let this be fair warning. If you do, I'll..." *jump your bones.* She swallowed. "Call the police."

"No, you won't."

"Oh, yes, I will."

She looked so adorable, Bryce thought. But, damn, he wished he knew why she kept fighting him. After their kiss today, Bryce was one-hundred percent positive the two of them were meant to be. She was the first woman who'd ever resisted him. Well, at least since he'd made it big in the children's toy industry. These days he could have any woman he wanted, and he didn't say that out of ego. He knew he wasn't a hunk. Boy next door. That's what more than one reporter had used to describe him. But that didn't stop women from flocking to his side—because of the money. That was the only reason. That and his sense of humor. Or so he told himself.

CJ was different.

Cute, sexy and one hell of a kisser. She wasn't impressed with his wealth. Gave him tit for tat, and she wasn't all caught up in wearing fashionable clothes or spotless makeup. In short, she was everything he'd been looking for in a woman, but didn't know he'd wanted...if that made sense. His heart softened when he touched her. He had an uncontrollable need to see her smile, to make her laugh.

He was falling for her.

As weird as it seemed having known her for just two days, he knew she had what it would take to make him sink...fast.

That was why he reached out and placed his hand on her thigh, happy to note that she jumped. "CJ, you could call the National Guard and that wouldn't keep me away."

"Oh, yeah?"

But her voice was just a squeak. If he kept up at it he could break down her wall of resistance. She may fight an emotional entanglement, but she couldn't fight the physical. And maybe that was the way to her heart, for suddenly he admitted to himself that he really *did* want her heart. Oh, yeah. He wanted to spoil her rotten. Wanted to take her on vacations where she'd never have to worry about rotten editors again. Wanted to see her eyes glow with happiness.

He navigated around a bend, glancing over at her. She stared out the window, a mutinous expression on her face.

"CJ, look, I know you don't think I'm the serious type. Hell, there are days when I don't take *myself* seriously. But you gotta believe me. There really is something between us."

She looked at him like she wanted to believe, but something held her back, some wound she didn't want picked at. What was it? Damn, he wished he knew.

"Bryce, I know you think what you feel for me is different, and it probably is..."

Damn straight it was.

"But I am different in looks, temperament, heck, probably even intelligence, but that doesn't make me different than any one of your other gal pals."

Gal pals?

"I'm sure every one of them thought they were the one for

you, and they were probably devastated when you dumped them—"

"Dumped them? I didn't dump anybody." Now he was losing his patience. She held up a hand. "All right. Went your separate ways. So while I appreciate your interest..."

He lifted a brow. *Appreciated?*

"Really," she added. "I'm flattered you've set your sights on me, but the fact is I don't want to be in someone's sights."

Especially yours, were the silent words.

He bit back an oath of frustration. Actually, he kinda liked that she didn't just jump in his arms. It was apparent he had his work cut out for him. Maybe he just needed to slow down, much as he hated to do that. But things were happening pretty fast between them. Maybe he should back off. They had time. All the time in the world.

He settled back in his seat, smiling. And if he couldn't break through, he'd kiss her senseless again. Hell, maybe he should do that anyway.

Chapter Nine

She didn't trust the look in his eyes, and so when her hour of purgatory finally ended, CJ wasted no time. She left the first check point as quickly as her asbestos-covered feet could carry her. It was a simple matter to bum a ride to the nearest town. From there she rented a car, but instead of driving to the next starting point she drove in the opposite direction—a two hour drive south—back to Las Vegas. It was a necessary task. Susan had invited her to visit Harmony Haven the day she'd met her and CJ had decided there was no time like the present to take her up on the offer. Unfortunately, she' d have to wait until later in the day to meet with her, but that was okay. By the time she drove back to the next staging area it'd be late at night

Perfect timing to avoid Bryce.

It meant hanging out in Vegas all day, but CJ didn't care. She would get started on writing her article and checking e-mails and doing anything else that would keep her busy and her mind off of Bryce.

And so it was nearly eight hours later when CJ finally pulled up in front of a lemon-colored home, a sign outside proclaiming the place to be Harmony Haven done in frilly, playful-looking letters. It didn't look like a foster home. It looked like a bed and breakfast. Gabled roof. Light gray roof tiles. A front porch that ran the length of the home. The town they were in was only a few miles away from where she and Bryce had started the off road rally race, but it seemed like an oasis. Hard to believe they were in the middle of the desert with the tall trees and green lawns that dotted the neighborhood.

"CJ," a little boy cried.

CJ's eyes moved to the bay window that was shielded by the porch's overhang. Daniel's excited face peered out at her, the little boy reminded her of a squirrel with the way he kept popping his head up.

"She's here," she heard him tell someone else inside the house.

"Good," a feminine voice answered. Susan? It must be.

Five seconds later she had her confirmation. The woman from the first day of the race called out a greeting. CJ automatically grinned back. Still, her feet felt like lead as she moved forward.

You're being ridiculous.

And she was. She knew that. Just because she didn't want to get involved with Bryce didn't mean she shouldn't use her journalistic connections to shine the light on one of his pet causes. What was wrong with her?

But she knew the answer to that too. It wasn't that she didn't want to write an article about Harmony Haven, it was that she didn't need another excuse to "like" Bryce. As it was, she "liked" him a little too much.

"Come in," the gray-haired woman said. "How was your drive?"

"Terrific," CJ said. It'd only taken her two hours to backtrack along state highways. To be honest, it'd felt nice to ride in a vehicle that didn't leave bruises on her shoulders.

"Sorry I couldn't meet with you this morning," the woman

said. "But there was a reason for the delay." She stepped aside.

"Hello, CJ."

The blood drained from her face.

"Isn't it great?" Daniel asked, bouncing up and down on the couch placed in front of the window. "He flew a helicopter here."

"A helicopter?" she repeated, more in shock than disbelief.

"I called him this morning and told him you wanted to meet with me. Imagine my surprise when Bryce told me he wanted to be here, too."

Good lord. She couldn't get cell service in her own backyard and yet the woman had actually gotten through to him in the middle of the desert. Was there no escaping the man?

CJ wanted to turn and walk out, but she knew she couldn't do that. "I see," she said instead.

"I thought it was important that I be here," he said. "I wanted to show you around some. Let you see what it's like for these kids."

She nodded, CJ making a big pretense of digging her camera out of the black nylon case she'd slung over her shoulder. But the image of him was burned into her mind. He wore street clothes. Light blue button down that hung out of his jeans. Freshly shaved too, by the looks of it. And showered. She could smell him all the way from where she stood.

"Okay," she said breathlessly. "Let's get started, shall we? Is it okay to take a picture of Daniel?" she asked Susan.

"Of course," the woman said with a smile in her bright, blue eyes.

What followed was an hour of sheer torture as she was forced to interact with Bryce. But not the Bryce from the race track. This was a new Bryce, one who was clearly on his best behavior. Nary a flirtatious glance flickered through his eyes. No lewd comments crossed his lips. He merely took her through the two story home—CJ becoming reacquainted with Marybeth, Samson, Patti and Laurie—CJ finding herself impressed by his speech despite trying to remain detached.

"This is what more big cities need to be doing," he said, motioning toward the play room they stood in. It was brightly lit thanks to a row of windows across the front of the house. Hardwood floors. Butter yellow walls. Cheery.

"A steady home for these kids to live in while they wait to be reunited with their moms and dads, or wait to be permanently placed," he said, tapping a toy car that had been left out with his toe, the thing skidding across the floor. "Instead, what happens is children are bounced from home to home. Handed off to perfect strangers instead of one individual."

"Someone like Susan," CJ provided.

"Yes," he said, nodding, smiling absently at the woman in question. "Susan does a great job, but she has help. Two other people work alongside of her, but it's always the same people. No sudden changes. That's what these kids need. Stability."

"You sound like you speak from experience."

She'd found very little information on Bryce's parents. She knew their names, but not much more.

"I do speak from experience," he said softly. "But not for the reasons you think," he said.

She lifted her brows in question.

"My parents fostered kids up until their death a few years ago."

He'd lost his parents?

"We always had a full house. It's how I ended up in the toy store business. I was always the kid playing around with things, trying to fix toys if they broke. Things wore out fast in our household and so my vocations sort of evolved out of necessity. The rest, as they say, is history."

She'd had no idea. Sure, she'd known he'd founded Toyco, but somehow she'd thought he hailed from a really rich family, one who'd given him a leg up to start his business. Obviously, that wasn't the case—not if there were worn toys laying around.

"But please don't print that," he said. "I don't want people digging into my past and bothering some of the kids I grew up with. They don't need that."

"No problem," she said, lifting her camera and taking a picture. Damn it, she'd known this would happen. She'd known sooner or later she'd end up with a whole new opinion of Bryce.

"Okay," she said brightly, too brightly. "I think I have enough." She turned to Susan. The blue-eyed lady smiled. "Thank you so much for agreeing to see me on such short notice."

"No problem," she said. "Anything for Bryce."

CJ steeled herself before meeting Bryce's eyes. "And thank you, Mr. Danvers," she said. "I'm sure you had to hustle to get here. The readers of *DRIVE Magazine* appreciate it."

"Are you going to tell them how much I love race cars?"

CJ spun around. Daniel stood there, a toothless smile on his face.

"And that Bryce let me ride in his race truck." He frowned a bit. "Well, not really. But he said that one day I could ride in one."

She squatted down before she could stop herself. He was adorable, this child. What was his story, she wondered. She hadn't wanted to pry. But it seemed impossible that someone had given him up for adoption.

He might have been taken away too.

She tried to keep the sadness from her eyes. "I promise the readers of *DRIVE* will get to read all about your off road racing adventures."

He smiled. CJ stood up before she did something silly, like pull the child into her arms.

"See you tomorrow, Bryce."

"No, wait," he said, "I'll walk you out."

She turned back in time to watch him give Susan a hug. "Thanks for everything."

"No, thank you," she said, hugging him back.

CJ looked away, pretending to fiddle with her camera when, in fact, all she succeeded in doing was shutting it off.

"Come on," Bryce said, lightly touching her arm so he could guide her down stairs.

Don't pull away, CJ. You'll look like an idiot if you do that.

"Lucky you gets to fly home," she said, trying to distract herself with conversation.

"You could fly home with me," he said softly.

This was the Bryce she knew. Bryce the flirt. Bryce the playboy. Frankly, she was grateful for his return. Bryce the good guy scared the crap out of her. It would be *so* easy to do something irresponsible with that man.

"That's okay," she said. "I have a rental car."

"You could leave it here."

They were at the head of a stairwell, CJ using the opportunity to break contact with him. She flew down the steps two at a time. "Thanks anyway," she called airily. "I'll just see you tomorrow."

"Bye, CJ," a little voice called.

Damn. She forced herself to stop. "Bye, Daniel," she said, smiling up at the boy before making a break for the door. Bryce caught up with her the moment her hand found the knob.

"We can have the rental car company pick it up. You could fly back home with me..."

Share my hotel room. And my bed... He didn't say the words out loud, but he didn't need to. She could read his unspoken intentions in his eyes.

"I have too much work to do."

Which was a stupid thing to say. It inferred that she'd have gone with him if it wasn't for the article she had to write.

"Do it in the morning," he said.

"No," she said firmly and with a lift of her chin. Mistake. It brought their lips closer together.

"You certain?" he asked, his gaze darting down, then back up again, the down again.

It was entirely too hot all of a sudden.

"Positive," she said.

"Darn," he murmured, and was she mistaken, or did his head drop a bit.

"Darn, what?" she found herself asking.

"That means I'll have to go to your hotel instead."

She drew back. "You wouldn't dare."

It was the wrong thing to say. She could tell he took her words as a challenge. "Oh, yes, I would."

No, he wouldn't. He was just pulling her leg.

Or was he?

He'd had no trouble tracking her down last night. "Bye, Bryce," she said, darting away before she said something else to provoke him.

"And so you just jumped into your rental car and drove away."

"Yup," CJ admitted to Deanna later that evening. "Although not without a few pit stops." Delaying tactics, she knew. She'd been hoping that if Bryce made good on his threats, he'd give up waiting for her. She'd been right, too, because when she'd finally pulled up in front of her hotel room a half-hour ago, the sun having long since faded from view, he'd been nowhere in sight.

Thank God.

"Good for you," Deanna said.

"Yeah, good for me," CJ repeated. She sat at the foot stool-sized table, her Powerbook open, flying toasters banding together to save her screen.

"How's the article coming?"

"Fantastic," CJ clipped out.

"That good, huh?"

CJ stabbed at her computer keys, wishing they were Miles's eyes. The toasters dissolved. Absently she started reading what she'd been typing prior to Deanna's call. "I'm working on the story right now. It's—" Her words halted abruptly as what she'd written formed into coherent sentences. She was horrified to note that she'd typed, for all the world to see, what it was like to have Bryce's hands on her body, what it felt like to have his lips against her own, worse, what it might feel like to make love to him. "Shit," she cursed.

"Shit?" Deanna questioned. "The article is shit?"

"No, no, no." CJ released an exasperated sigh. "You wouldn't believe me if I told you."

"I don't know. If you've been reduced to swearing, it must be pretty good."

"It isn't. Listen. I should prob—" A knock sounded out. "—get going," she finished vaguely.

"What's wrong?" bionic eared Deanna asked.

"Someone's knocking on my door."

"'Bout time he got there."

"Stop it."

Deanna clucked like a chicken. CJ rolled her eyes.

That was when CJ heard the voice on the other side of the door. "CJ?"

CJ stiffened. Why that had sounded like—

"CJ, it's me, Kathleen Seavers."

She sat up, feeling a rush of disappointment. *Kathleen?* What the heck was she doing here this late at night?

She clutched the phone tighter before saying, "Deanna, I've got to go. I think she's at my door."

"She?"

"The woman I caught in Bryce's arms today."

"What!"

CJ ignored her. "I gotta go." She hung up the phone, but not before she could hear Deanna's irate voice screeching across the line.

Tip-toeing over to the window, she pulled the curtains aside a scant inch. It *was* Kathleen. Svelte and glamorous in jeans, white cotton shirt, and a black leather vest. CJ released the drape and went over to the door. She was just about to swing it wide when sudden suspicion made her peek out a small gap. "Is he with you?"

"Oh good, you *are* here," Kathleen said, smiling at her in an all too friendly way. "He who?"

"Bryce, that's who."

"Bryce? Nope. Not here."

CJ released a sigh of relief—or was it disappointment—and opened the door. "I thought this might be a set up."

"It *is* a set up," said an all too familiar masculine voice.

CJ stiffened, caught sight of Bryce out of the corner of her eye, yelped like a poodle being stepped on, and tried to slam the door. It didn't work due to a size twelve foot. CJ was tempted to ram it closed but she was never one to retreat. So she placed her hands on her hips and gave him a look meant to singe the hair off his head.

He ignored it and sauntered into the room, smiling at her like a fly on a compost heap. She supposed she could tell him to leave, but it would apparently make no difference. The whole situation had gotten out of hand. Kathleen had already skulked away. CJ slammed the door behind her and glared at Bryce.

"How in the heck did you get my room number?"

He smiled deviously. "I slipped the guy at the front desk a hundred bucks."

"The little creep. I gave him twenty *not* to give it to you."

"Let that be a lesson to you. I'd pay any price to see you."

She tried to ignore the little tingles his words evoked, just as she tried to ignore his presence, but that was like trying to stop an avalanche with a butterfly net. He wore the same light-blue button-down as before, a shirt that exactly matched the color of his eyes. His jeans hugged his frame in a way Levi Strauss would give its third quarter profits to duplicate. His skin, tanned from his many hours in the sun, gave off that tangy, foresty aroma she'd become addicted to. She resisted the urge to close her eyes and inhale.

"I'm here to keep my promise, CJ," he whispered in a voice so soft it sent another jolt of adrenaline through her. God help her, she knew in that instant that she'd been kidding herself. She'd been hoping he wouldn't give up. That he'd wait for her to show up. That he'd want to see her so badly, he'd track her down once again.

He had.

The look in his eyes intensified, turned a color as deep as sapphires.

But she couldn't let this happen. Not tonight. Not ever.

Bryce took a step toward her, watching as her eyes widened almost imperceptibly. She looked so cute in her jeans and pink T-shirt. No makeup covered the slight dusting of freckles on her cheeks and her pert little nose. Her mahogany-colored hair lay loose about her shoulders in rumpled disarray, as if she'd run her fingers through it a time or two, he'd guess in frustration by the look in her eyes. Poor CJ. She had no idea the time for running was over.

"Would it be too much to ask you to leave?"

"Yes."

"Fine, then *I'm* leaving," she snapped.

"Not before we talk."

"Talk? About what?"

"About how it's going to feel when I when I make love to you."

She stiffened. So did he, though not his back.

"Oh no," she said, raising her hand in the air. "No, no, no. I'm not going to have this conversation."

He took a step toward her, growing harder by the second. "Which conversation? The one about how I'm going to strip your clothes off and taste every inch of your body?"

"Stop it," she repeated, retreating a step, her back bumping up against the wall.

"I don't want to stop, CJ. I want you to admit what there is between us."

"I'm not listening," she plugged her ears and closed her eyes, humming the National Anthem.

He tried not to laugh. "I know you can hear me."

"What?" she yelled. "Did you say something?"

"And I know you want me. I know you feel what's between us." He took the last final step, a step toward the commitment, toward the future. She was so cute the way she kept denying their attraction to each other, but her eyes, her eyes said it all. They burned with heat, sent white-hot electricity leaping through his veins. If he could just de-activate the too-active brain of hers for a second...

Her hands dropped from her ears. She looked like she was about to bolt so he reached out and gently cupped her chin. Her skin was so smooth, so soft. "Do you *really* want me to leave?" She smelled like passion and promises.

He saw her swallow, saw the emotions in her eyes; confusion, fear...want. "Yes."

"Really?"

She nodded, but the expression on her face told him the opposite. She looked like a little sex kitten, all hot and feisty. And so he tested her words by bending down and gently kissing her. Her eyes widened just before his lips connected. She was unyielding at first, then suddenly her mouth opened to his. She tasted like toothpaste; minty and sweet.

She pulled away quickly, as if she couldn't believe she'd let him kiss her. Her cheeks were flushed, her chest heaved, her green eyes swimming with tempestuous anger and something else.

"Don't you ever do that again," she snapped. And then she grabbed him by the back of the neck, pulled his head down and kissed him back.

Bryce was too surprised to do much more than stand there, but the feel of her pressed against him, the taste of her flooding his mouth again—the very fact that *she* was the aggressor—had him begging for more.

Desire burst between them like steam from a radiator. Her body began to tremble, and he knew she felt the same thing he did. Soft moans rose from her throat. Her skin burned, even through the fabric of her shirt, and suddenly the cotton shirt was a nuisance. His hand fumbled at the waist of her jeans, tugging, jerking, lifting the shirt up high enough to place his fingers against her side. And when his fingers made contact with her breast she stiffened, then retreated against the wall again.

"Don't," she ordered firmly.

"Don't stop?" He knew good and well what she meant; but he couldn't seem to quit touching her.

"Don't do this." And then she pulled his shirt out of his waistband, and this time it was his turn to moan as she touched him, slid her nails up his abdomen, over his ribcage, circling his nipple once before burying her fingers in the hair on his chest.

"God, CJ." He cupped her breast in his hand, using his other hand to release the catch on her bra. Magnificent, more than a handful, soft to the touch, her nipple a hard pebble in his palm. He wanted to taste that nipple, wanted to suck it until those soft moans rose in her throat again. He leaned toward her, placing his palm against the wall and tugging her closer with his other hand. She tensed. Then his lips captured a pebbled nub and she melted in his arms.

"Oh jeez," she whispered. "Oh jeez, oh jeez, oh jeez."

He swirled a circle with his tongue. She arched her back like a cat, offering herself to him, rubbing against him. Damn, he was going to pop, was going to explode inside his pants like some adolescent boy. He couldn't believe the effect she had on him. It was like driving Harry's truck off the edge of a cliff; exhilarating, wild, mind-blowing and it was only when she started moaning again that he stopped, drawing away from her reluctantly.

"Get undressed, honey."

She shook her head, her eyes closed. "I...I don't think that's such a good idea."

"It's all right," he reassured, gently stroking the side of her face, and then bending down to trail kisses along the column of her neck.

"It's not a pretty sight," she mumbled.

"I can take it." He lightly bit her ear lobe.

"Oh, man," she moaned.

He continued to nibble. "C'mon, honey."

"It's too ugly."

He reached between them. "What is?" he asked, hardly aware of what she was saying, far more interested in undoing her jeans.

"My body."

Her words suddenly registered, disbelief making him draw back in surprise. Her eyes were filled with so much uncertainty and anxiety and doubt that his heart lurched against his chest. That CJ, his calm, confident, brave CJ should be so insecure about her body made his heart swell. "Ah, CJ, honey. You have a beautiful body."

But the expression on her face told him she didn't believe him.

"You do," he reaffirmed.

"You don't need to pretend with me."

He couldn't believe it. She sounded like a martyr.

"Look," he said firmly, lifting her shirt. He almost groaned, instead he forced himself to say, "Do you see this?" cupping a breast and weighing it in his palm. "*This*," he went on, ignoring her gasp and the painful throbbing in his groin, "is the most beautiful breast I've ever seen."

She tried to draw away.

"Don't you believe me?"

"Oh, I don't doubt it's more than a mouthful," she muttered, looking up at him dubiously.

"Perfect," he clarified, reluctantly letting go. "And your skin is soft and smooth. It's like the most supple of leather car seats."

"Oh great," she mumbled. "Just what I want. Naugahide breasts."

"Do you know how much I want to kiss that skin, to touch you everywhere?" He demonstrated by lightly stroking her abdomen.

"No," she moaned.

"And your butt. God, CJ, it's amazing. Perfectly formed, heart-shaped. Whenever you walk away from me I can't stop staring at it. And your legs. I go crazy just thinking about them wrapped around me." He gently turned her head and forced her to look at him, his voice firm as he said, "I want to bury myself inside of you."

"Oh jeez," she whispered.

Emotions overtook him as he stared down at her; tenderness, amusement...anger. Who was the bastard who had done this to her, made her so insecure? Whoever he was, the man should be shot.

"Bryce," she said his name softly, almost in wonder. "You better not be lying."

He chuckled, couldn't seem to stop himself, then pulled her up against him. "Come, here, you little idiot. Let me prove to you just how much your body pleases me." He clasped her hand in his and guided it to his erection. "Do you feel that?" And when she nodded, he dipped his head down to nuzzle her ear. "That's what you do to me." She pulled her hand away, but he guided it back. "Touch me, CJ. I'm begging."

He counted the seconds of her hesitation. After two seconds he closed his eyes.

By four he felt her hand on his button down fly.

By six she was stroking the length of him.

By eight he almost came. All she did was run her hand up his hardness, the fabric of his jeans shielding him from her touch, but it could have been her lips that stroked him, could have been her sweet tongue licking him. His whole body jerked, unfurled like a coiled spring. "Ahh, CJ, honey, do it again."

She did.

He groaned, then dipped his head down to nibble at her ear again. He couldn't seem to get enough of her, wanted to lap up the taste of her for the rest of his life. His lips traveled lower; along the cord of her neck. He lifted her shirt to the top of her breast. She arched into him; he swirled his tongue around her nipple.

"Bryce. Yes, Bryce, please..." Her hand flexed and tightened against him.

Her nipple shrunk, became a hardened tip in his mouth. He sucked on it, played with it with his tongue.

"Yes, Bryce, that's it."

She was going to be the death of him. He just knew it.

"Let's move to the bed." He felt her stiffen, then draw away "CJ?"

"I have to...I have to," She panted, her green eyes smoky, her hair in wild disarray. "I have to get the door," she finished in a rush.

Door? What door? Ah shit. Someone *was* knocking on the damn door.

She was out of his arms before he could stop her, his body left revving like a motor at the starting line with the race canceled.

"You ordered pizza?" asked a pimply faced youth with a red, white and blue baseball cap on his head, his left hand scratching his left armpit and his right hand carried a pizza box. Extra large.

"Yeah," CJ rasped out, her breath as fast as a rabbit fleeing for its life. Dang, what had almost happened?

You just about peeled Bryce's banana, that's what almost happened. Way to keep your distance, Ceej. Next you'll be pulling off your clothes off, screaming, "Let me be your sex goddess".

The kid pulled out a receipt, balancing the cardboard box in his other hand. "Okay. It comes to $16.95."

"Huh?" She blinked, then forced herself to concentrate. "Ahh, yeah, right. $16.85."

"Ninety-five," the kid corrected. "Did you want peppers or— holy shit."

"Um, I'll pass on the shit," CJ mumbled, fumbling in her

pocket for the twenty she'd stuffed in her jeans.

"You're that kid's toy store king guy."

CJ darted a glance behind her.

"In the flesh," Bryce drawled in lazy syllables.

"Wow!" the kid exclaimed, "I've seen your commercials." He turned toward her. "Are you somebody?" he asked, looking at her excitedly; as if she had to be somebody to be in the presence of such a pseudo-celebrity.

"She's my girlfriend," Bryce answered for her.

"Your girlfriend?" the kid blurted. "*She's* your girlfriend?" He said it like, "This brown haired, overweight, Orca-the-Killer-Whale look-alike is your *girlfriend*?" CJ wanted to conk him over the head with his pizza box. Okay so she wasn't much to look at, she could admit that, wasn't even bothered by it on most days, but she didn't need to be reminded that she wasn't Bryce's usual type by some kid with acne medicine spackled all over his face, especially in light of her and Bryce's recent conversations. She stuffed the twenty in the brat's greasy hand.

"I'm not his girlfriend, I'm a journalist." She looked back at Bryce with a glare that warned him he best keep his mouth shut. Which he did. Smart man.

"Oh, I see. He was joking."

The little shit pocketed the whole twenty without bothering to make change. CJ put her hand out. The kid gave her the evil eye. She arched a brow. He reached into his pocket, slapping down some ones and her change in her watery palm.

"Never insult the lady who ordered the pizza," CJ said sweetly, jamming the notes and coins into her front pocket.

Ignoring her, the kid turned to Bryce and said, "Hey, can I have your autograph? I was going to go out to the race tomorrow, but it'd be great if you could sign one now."

"Well isn't that neat, Bryce? He wants your autograph," CJ said, seeing a way to get rid of Bryce, for suddenly it was imperative she do so, imperative because she knew if she let him make love to her it'd be the biggest mistake of her life. Bigger than Ed, even. Any other man who came into her life would pale in comparison to Bryce.

She deposited her pizza on a nearby table and grabbed Bryce by the arm, forcing him toward the door. "Why don't you go on down to his car and sign one for him?"

"Wow, would you?" the kid exclaimed. "That'd be great."

She got Bryce as far as the doorway before he put on the brakes. "CJ, I'm sure you've got a piece of paper in here I can sign."

"In here? Don't be silly, Bryce. Even Gideon hasn't been here." She dragged him forward another step.

He dug in his heels. "I'm not leaving this room."

She pushed harder. "Oh, yes, you are."

He leaned into her. "No, I'm not."

"Ahh," the kid said, "I can wait to get the autograph tomorrow."

They both turned to look at the boy who was staring at them like they'd suddenly announced they were Gorts from the evil planet Zoltar.

"No need to do that," she said, giving him her best fake smile. She turned back to Bryce. "I'll make you a deal. We'll wait right here for this nice young man to fetch a piece of paper for you to sign."

Bryce stared at her suspiciously before saying, "Fine."

They looked at the kid. "Go on," CJ said, shooing him with her hand.

The boy turned away. CJ waited until he got as far as the

stairwell before making her move.

With all her might she gave Bryce a huge shove.

"Hey," he cried, stumbling out the door.

She closed it in his face.

"Damn it, CJ, why'd you do that?" he called from the other side.

Deanna was right, she was a chicken. But she was a chicken with a healthy dose of self-preservation.

"CJ, I'm not leaving until you and I talk."

The kid was right. She wasn't Bryce's type. Better to realize that now before he discovered the red dent around her waist where her jeans dug in. But, damn it, it took every ounce of self-control to keep the door closed. She groaned, heading toward the bathroom without a second thought. She needed a shower. A cold one. Now.

"Damn it," Bryce muttered from the other side of the door.

"You want me to try?" the freckle-faced kid asked.

Bryce stared down at him impatiently. It was hot outside. The motel was the kind with a long balcony, wrought iron railing keeping guests from falling into the parking lot below. But he had a feeling the heat he felt had more to do with the woman on the other side of the door than the waning sunlight.

"No," he said morosely, wondering what to do. If he knocked on the door again she'd just ignore him. That he knew beyond a shadow of a doubt. And she hadn't opened the window next to the motel room door. And he refused to drag Kathleen into this again. He already felt bad for involving her the first time around.

"I have a friend that works here."

Bryce turned toward the kid quickly. He was nodding, his

pimples standing out in stark contrast to his white skin even in the gray light.

"Do you now?" Bryce asked.

The teenager nodded, his Adam's apple bobbing. "He cleans rooms here. I bet he could keep an eye out for her. You know, in case she leaves or something."

But Bryce was toying with another idea, one that had instantly sprung to mind. "I don't think she's going to go anywhere tonight."

"No?" the kid asked, obviously disappointed.

"So we need to do something different. Something a little more inventive."

But Bryce didn't trust that CJ wasn't listening at the door, so he led the kid away, to the stairwell not more than twenty feet from CJ's room, and then down the stairs. "A 'you scratch my back and I'll scratch yours' type of thing," Bryce added.

The kid tipped his head back. He really did have a lot of pimples, especially when his face came out from beneath the shadow of his ball cap. "I'm not sure I'd be comfortable with doing something too different," the kid admitted.

"Yeah, but have you ever wanted to go on a shopping spree?" Bryce asked, throwing out the bait. "At a store that carries the largest selection of video games in the nation?"

The boy's face lit up. "Yeah."

"I'll let you and your friend do exactly that, but here's what you have to do for me."

He was gone. She'd watched him walk down the steps with the pizza kid. CJ jerked the drapes closed, a part of her bitterly and ridiculously disappointed that he wasn't holding down the fort right outside her door.

Of course he isn't going to do that, CJ. That's called stalking, and he's already stalked you one too many times today. Jeez. Forget about the man. She tried to, contented herself with working on her article instead which, miraculously enough, didn't take her all that long to complete. It wasn't hard to write about Bryce. Not when there was so much to talk about. She shared with readers his sense of humor. Described the way he interacted with children. She even admitted that he wasn't half-bad of a driver, and that when it came right down to it, she was having the adventure of her life.

One that would end all too soon.

She tried not to think about that. Instead, two hours later she pulled back the covers of her bed and gave herself free reign to have some crazy-hot wet dreams about the man.

That's exactly what happened too. In her dream, Bryce slipped into bed next to her. But unlike the previous night's dreams, she didn't want to play hard to get. So she just laid there—still—every nerve ending in her body zinging to life. But what the hell. This was a dream, right? She could do whatever she damn well pleased. So when Bryce scooted closer to her, when she heard him softly whisper her name, she turned to face him and said the words she'd kept bottled up inside.

"Take me."

And it was such a realistic experience that she thought she heard his breath catch, thought she heard him moan. "Ah, honey. I was hoping you'd say that."

He pulled her close to him. She sighed and when, a heartbeat later, he kissed her, she instantly opened her mouth to him. That's what fantasies were all about: doing something you'd never do in real life. And so she flicked her tongue into his mouth, invited him to delve deeper, to taste her more fully. He did, and suddenly she couldn't get enough of him. He couldn't, either, and they were both moaning as he covered her body with his own.

She almost woke up then.

It took everything she had not to let that happen. She arched her body into him, hoping to recapture the amazing way it felt to have him up against her. To know that Bryce Danvers was in her bed. Making love to her. Stroking her. Tasting her. She felt his hand move between their bodies.

And she was lost again.

His fingers skated beneath her sleep shirt. She never wore underwear to bed and so she knew he'd find bare skin down there. Her woman's mound tingled in anticipation. Those tingles turned into a heat as his fingers moved closer and closer to her center.

Yes!

This was what fantasies were all about. This was what she'd imagined as she'd sat next to him in the race truck. She wanted it. Didn't hesitate before parting her legs to him.

He touched her.

She sighed. His finger slid down her valley at the same time his tongue slipped deeper into her mouth. She pushed against his hand. Opened her mouth even more, wanting all of him. Now.

He broke the kiss off.

"No," she cried. But his lips had found her neck and she settled into the bed again, her body feeling heavy, her limbs splayed in all direction. The only things that moved were her toes. With every kiss, they curled in delight.

"Bryce, I think I'm going to die."

She felt his chest vibrate against her side. He was lifting her shirt now and she knew he would suckle her breast. Her nipples hardened in anticipation. When his teeth lightly grazed the sensitive tips, she moaned again. And when he drew his hand up her suddenly slick center, she truly thought she might die...of pleasure.

His tongue mimicked the motion of his fingers. She'd begun to writhe beneath him because she really didn't want his lips on her breast. She wanted his mouth there...where his hand was, her most wicked of all fantasies and something she'd never experienced before. She'd wanted men to do that to her. The closest she'd come was teeth lightly grazing the mound of her jeans. But she wanted the real deal. She wanted his tongue. His lips. His mouth to suckle her and God help her, he seemed willing to comply.

"Yes," she hissed again, her stomach twitching when his lips found the sensitive spot above her belly button. He swirled his tongue around it. She cried out in pleasure. And then...and then...oh, dear Lord, he was there. Right there, at her opening.

"Spread your legs for me."

She'd already done that. Hadn't she? But no. Modesty had kept her thighs close together. Only he wanted all of her, demanded unhindered access, took matters into his own hands by sliding his arms beneath her thighs and pulling her up against his mouth.

"Bryce," she cried out again.

She almost climaxed right then. He wouldn't let her. The wretch knew exactly what he was doing with her because he didn't cup her with his mouth. Oh, no, he teased her with his tongue, flicked the tip of it against the nub of her sensitivity so that her whole body tightened—a near release—only to have him draw back before she could slip over the edge.

Bastard.

But it was so damn good. Felt so damn incredible. She

wanted the moment to go for eternity. And he was good at it. So damn good at bringing her there—right there—before retreating a bit so that she didn't fall over the edge.

"You taste so good," she heard him mutter.

Her body spasmed in response. "Do I?" she heard herself ask on a breathless whisper.

"I want to taste your come."

She moaned. Wicked, wicked man. She wanted him to taste her. Wanted to give all of herself to him.

"Take me, Bryce," she panted. "Now."

"No," he said.

But the protest she'd been about to utter was cut off when his tongue slipped inside her. *Deep* inside her.

"Oh, God."

He wasn't playing anymore. Oh, no. The time for games appeared to be over because his mouth suckled every inch of her and she knew she would climax in a matter of seconds, but that was okay because this was a dream and she could do whatever she damn well wanted even if she'd never done anything so wanton in her life. And so she lifted herself up on her elbow so she could watch herself come in his mouth.

Watch herself?

Yes, watch herself. Because when she opened her eyes she knew this was no dream.

That was Bryce down there. Bryce who looked up at her, his face clearly illuminated by the clock radio. Bryce's eyes that stared into her own.

"Crap."

But she didn't care. If anything knowing it was him, really him, heightened her pleasure.

"Come," he ordered.

She was lifting her hips now. Urging him on. If he wanted her, by God he would have her. All of her. She would flood his mouth with her pleasure. Let him taste all of her.

She screamed.

She didn't mean to, thought at first it must be someone else, recognized her own voice when she cried, "Bryce, oh, God, Bryce. Yessssss."

She'd never, not ever, had a climax like Bryce gave her. It was every orgasm she'd ever had all rolled into one, her body tightening and then pulsing, the hairs on her neck seeming to stand on end.

And still he suckled her.

"Give me another one," she heard him say.

No. Impossible. She couldn't possibly climax again. The touch of his mouth seemed nearly painful now.

And yet...

She still moved her hips, still gave him access. "Another one?" she huffed.

"Yes."

And so she did, and this time she nearly doubled over from the force of her body's violent release. She screamed again. Ripples of pleasure rocketed through her body. She flopped back on the bed, cried out his name again and again.

"I knew you'd be like this," Bryce told her when she came back to earth. Man, he had the biggest hard-on of his life. He couldn't wait until it was his turn.

"Like what?" he heard her ask.

"Hot." He was leaning back on his elbows now. "The hottest

woman I've ever been in bed with."

He knew it was the wrong thing to say the moment the words left his mouth. If he could have snatched them back, he would have. She scooted up on her elbows again. "Excuse me?" she said.

"I didn't mean that the way it sounded."

"No?"

"I mean, we're obviously not virgins. We've both had sex before. There's nothing wrong with that."

He was only making things worse.

"You broke into my room," she said, rolling away from him and clicking on the light next to the bed.

"CJ, wait. Don't do that." Damn it. How had it gone so wrong? In so short an amount of time.

"Just exactly how did you get into my room?" she asked, jerking the covers up around her as if he hadn't just made her scream his name in pleasure.

"I bribed the pizza guy."

"Excuse me?"

He shook his head. "It doesn't matter. I figured that if you didn't really want me in your room, you'd boot me out. Like you did yesterday."

"*I thought it was a dream,*" she cried. "All of it. You crawling into bed with me. Your kisses. That thing you did."

"It was good, wasn't it?"

She glared.

"Come on," he said, sitting up too. He was still fully clothed and he wouldn't be at all surprised if he didn't bust the crotch out of his jeans. She glanced down as if reading his thoughts, her gaze quickly sliding away from the evidence of his arousal.

"Come on, CJ. You couldn't have been asleep for all of it."

She didn't respond, just pressed her lips together before saying, "You should leave."

"Now? After what we just did together."

"I'm calling security."

"CJ, no. Don't," he said, scooting off the bed. She glared up at him looking for all the world like a irate princess with a gown of bedspread falling around her. "Look, I'm sorry for breaking into your room." He ran a hand through his hair. "I know that was a brazen thing to do. But I honestly thought after that kiss we shared earlier..."

"That I'd fall into your arms."

He found himself nodding even though he knew it was a dumb idea. "Something like that."

"Congratulations. You were right. Now leave."

"Damn it, CJ. It doesn't have to be this way. What's wrong with having an affair?"

He saw her chest rise, knew he'd said the wrong thing...again. "Because that's all it would ever be," she said, slipping from the bed, the night shirt she wore falling around her waist. "An affair. One that could get me fired." She crossed to the door. "Thank you for, um, joining me in bed—"

"And making you come?" he couldn't resist saying.

She blushed.

"But I need you to leave now," she said, ignoring her words.

"CJ—"

"Now," she added, and he could tell she meant it.

Damn it.

He shot up from the bed. CJ opened the door. "You're making a mistake," he said.

"Actually," he heard her say, "this is one of the smartest things I've done in my life."

Chapter Ten

The next morning CJ arrived at the race twenty minutes before it was due to start. It was cutting it close, she admitted, but she didn't want to risk running into Bryce. She took a deep, fortifying breath of dry, desert air and tried to quell the need to puke. She couldn't believe what had happened last night. Couldn't believe Bryce had snuck into her room. Couldn't believe she'd have to face him again. After he'd done that to her.

Dear God, would the torture never end?

She'd made it through two days...and she had the bruises to prove it, but now she'd have to deal with a whole new type of torment. Bryce. And the memory of what he'd done to her.

It's only for one more hour.

But tomorrow it would be all over. Today would be the last day of fending off Mr. Playboy of America; the last day of putting up with his machinations; the last day of fantasizing about what it would be like to make love to him. Check that. She'd already done made love to him. Or he'd made love to her. Damn it. She didn't want to think about it. "There you are, CJ," Harry said as she arrived at the transporter.

The team owner was standing in the middle of the isle, a clipboard in his right hand, a Styrofoam cup in his left and a frown on his face large enough to rival the losing politician on Election Day.

"Morning, Harry," she answered back.

"Have you seen Bryce?"

"I just got here."

"He's not with you?"

"No. Why would you think that?" she asked suddenly, quickly and entirely too guiltily.

"Well, he's bangin' ya, ain't he?"

The barometer on CJ's mood scale went to negative. "No, Mr. Santini, he is not."

Almost.

Shut up, she told herself.

Harry's jowls hung beneath his slack jaw like gills on a frog. "No?"

She set her jaw and shook her head.

"Humph. I wonder where he is then."

"I've been in jail."

CJ stiffened.

"Bryce, damn it," Harry said, looking past her shoulder. "You weren't D&D, were you? If they've pulled your license—"

"No, Harry. Prior to my arrest, bumping and grinding would be a more adequate description of what I was doing, but that's not what I was arrested for."

CJ choked

"What the hell happened?" Harry snapped.

"Why don't you ask Miss Randall here?"

Slowly, CJ turned around. "Me?" she said, pointing to her chest. "What'd I have to do with your getting locked up?"

The glint in Bryce's eyes was positively glacial. "Did you call the hotel manager after I left your room?"

"Last night?" she asked, playing dumb.

He took a small step toward her. "Yes, CJ, last night. Right after you slammed the door in my face. And right after that *other* thing happened."

Retreat, screamed her brain, but she held her ground. The last time she'd retreated it hadn't done any good. "Um. I might have. I don't really recall. Last night was such a blur."

"Oh, really," he asking, taking another step toward her. "Well, let me jog your memory. After you called the night manager and told them some weirdo tried to peek into your room, he apparently called the police."

Her eyes widened. "I thought they'd ask you to leave."

"I was about to do exactly that when the manager waylaid me and asked me what I was doing there. I told him you and I were friends."

"Let me guess. He didn't believe you."

"No, CJ, because you wouldn't answer your door. And my wallet must have fallen out in your hotel room—"

Uh oh.

"—because I didn't have any ID on me, and they needed you to identify me after I claimed you and I were friends. They knocked on your door for ten minutes."

"I was in the shower," CJ explained, washing off the scent of him.

"Why didn't you call me?" Harry asked looking between the two like they were participants in a tennis match.

"I did. You didn't answer your cell phone."

"You should have tried the satellite phone."

Bryce's expression turned, if possible, even more heated. "I didn't even know you had one. It'd be nice if I had the number," he shot before his gaze lanced back to hers. "And when you didn't answer *your* phone, you know what they did?"

"Took you to the DMV to check your identity?"

One more step, and now he was only inches away. "No, they decided to hold me in a cell overnight until someone came down to bail me out."

"How could they do that? Wouldn't I have to press charges or something?"

"*Not* if the arresting officer is Barney Fife."

CJ's brows rose. "Did you call him that?"

"I did."

She lifted a brow. "Then it serves you right."

"Serves me right? None of this would have happened if you hadn't called the manager in the first place..."

He sounded *very* frustrated, CJ observed.

"Ahem," Harry interrupted, both heads swung toward him. "How'd you get out, son?"

"Another officer recognized me, but the guy didn't come in until five o'clock this morning." Bryce turned back to her. "Do you know how bad it smells in jail?"

"As bad as your race helmet?" she asked with false sympathy.

He leaned close to her. "No, as bad as Harry's shoes."

"Hey," Harry protested.

They both ignored him. "Gee, Bryce. I'm, ahh, I'm really sorry." And she was. She really, really was.

He moved his head even closer, his lips only inches away. "You can show me how *sorry* you are in private."

"No, she can't," Harry interjected. "You guys are due at the starting line in ten minutes."

Bryce straightened away, but it was evident in the way he

looked at her that he wasn't finished. Not by a long shot. CJ gulped.

The jerk waited until they were right next to his truck before making his first move. CJ yelped as he tugged her around and kissed her in front of the fans, Harry's pit crew, the TV cameras, God and everyone. But what really made her mad was that her whole body started to tingle; from the tips of her Mechanix shoes to the roots of her split-ended hair. Suddenly she couldn't remember what it was they were fighting about. All she could recall was the way his lips had felt against her skin last night. And how wonderfully he'd brought her to a climax. And how badly she wanted to experience the sensations all over again. He tasted sweet, like donuts, and when he drew away she almost grabbed him by the back of his head and forced him to do it again. For a long minute all she did was stare up at him, ignoring the fans who were hooting and whistling at their display.

Bryce ignored them too. "You know, I was thinking this morning," he said, his lips still only inches away.

She couldn't take her eyes off of them. "Is *that* where all that smoke came from?"

He ignored her. "I was thinking how a jail cell would be the perfect place to make love to you, smells and all. You know, no phones, no Harry, no pizza boys...no way for you to boot me out. But then I thought, wait, why would I want to make love to a woman on a cold, hard, smelly jail bed when I could make love to her in the middle of the desert instead?"

She jerked away, suddenly remembering they were supposed to be fighting. When she took a step back she summoned what few brain cells his kiss hadn't sucked out and said, "Don't you think Harry might have something to say about stopping his truck to enact some sort of petty revenge? You're already slowing things down by stopping to let me out after an hour."

"What makes you think we're stopping to let you out today?" he asked.

"Bryce," she said warningly. He had to be kidding.

"Oh it won't be petty," he said smugly. "And Harry'd want to watch."

She colored, her face glowing as brightly as the taillights on Bryce's truck.

"You forget about the business he's in."

No. She remembered.

"Go ahead and mount up," Harry said from right behind her, and his timing couldn't have been more superb.

CJ turned toward the man, horrified that he'd overheard. Then she spotted Harry pointing at the truck. Her face turned redder. Bryce chuckled. "I wanted to do exactly that last night," he murmured in her ear. "But you wouldn't let me." He drew back. "Maybe I'll have better luck today."

She was seized by the thoroughly childish urge to stomp on his foot. "I'm getting out after an hour," she said.

"C'mon, you two. We've only got a few minutes to get this thing to the starting line."

Bryce leaned forward, placing a hand on her shoulder. "C'mon, CJ," he whispered in her ear. "It's time to head off into the desert."

"Not without a cattle prod, I'm not," she hissed back.

"A cattle prod, hmm. That might be kind of fun. I'm sure Harry has one...or something close."

"You're twisted."

"Not as twisted as a woman who calls the cops on her lover."

CJ turned back to face him. "You're not my lover."

"Oh, no? That wasn't you screaming my name last night?"

"I didn't scream."

"No?"

"I moaned," she clarified.

"Ah. Well, those were some of the loudest moans I've ever heard."

She blushed because she really had made a lot of noise. "And I did not call the cops on you."

"That's what you say, but in hindsight, the manager never admitted that he was the one who called the police. I wouldn't put it past you to pull a fast one like that."

"I didn't pull a fast one, I merely showed you to the door." And she hadn't called the police. She really hadn't.

Someone waved a hand between them. It was Harry. "Are you going to help her into the truck or shall I get out the crane?"

"I will," Bryce announced at the same time CJ muttered, "Jerk," under her breath.

Bryce grabbed her right beneath her breast, copping a quick feel as he supposedly helped her up the step ladder that sat beneath the sill of the truck. CJ closed her eyes and tried not to notice the tingles his fingers sent through her whole body as she slid into her seat, silently cursing.

"Let's see," Bryce mused as he strapped himself in next to her a moment later. "I guess I'll wait until Devil's Bones to pull over. Do you mind waiting that long? Of course, it could be sooner, but I like the name. It has a certain ring to it, wouldn't you say? Kinda memorable. And it reminds me of last night, you know, when I left your room with a huge boner."

"Don't be crass," she snapped. CJ checked to make sure there were no stray *things* attached to her belt and said, "I'm sorry you were left, ah, hanging like that, but that's no reason to force me into riding along all day."

"It was very definitely *not* hanging," he said. "And I thought you were supposed to ride along all day."

"I've changed my mind." She put in her ear pieces even though the last thing she wanted was Bryce's voice in her ear all day. "But you know, you and Harry ought to get together and exchange euphemisms. Maybe you can help him name his products."

Bryce considered her suggestion as she leaned back in her seat and crossed her arms over her painfully hard nipples. "That's a great idea. He'd probably like what you called it last night. What was it? Little Bryce?"

"I said no such thing."

"Or was it Big Bryce?"

"You must've been hearing things. If I called it anything it was the Teeny Weeny."

"Teeny Weeny? Hardly. More like Whoppin' Weeny."

She snorted in disdain. "Yeah right."

"Or maybe it was Pleasure Pumper."

"How about Pencil Pecker?"

"Or Whopper Wanger?"

"And how about you two move it to the starting line?" Harry interrupted.

CJ looked outside in horror. Bryce's crew stared at them both, all of them grinning from ear-to-ear, except for Harry, who frowned. "Ohmigosh," she screeched, clutching the window sill. "You opened the mic, didn't you?"

Bryce smiled.

"*You*, you, you," words failed her. "You *bastard*. You total and complete *bastard*."

"Bryce," Harry interjected, barely able to control his laughter. "You better close that mic before the FCC fines us."

"Roger, Harry," Bryce said, moving the switch on his steering wheel into the off position. "Did you pull your harness tight? I don't want any more bruises sprouting up on your shoulders."

"What do you care?"

He smiled. A cat-in-a-fish-store kind of smile. "My, my, my. We're in quite a snit, aren't we? Could it be because now everyone knows you and I have been intimate?"

"We have *not* been intimate."

"But we will be...soon."

"Yeah, over my dead, bloated and decomposed body."

"That's not what you said last night."

"Well, you can forget all about last night. Besides, today's the last day of the race. I hardly think you're going to jeopardize your chances of winning by pulling over to exact some type of revenge."

"You're wrong."

She glared at him dubiously.

"You see, I don't want to win the race."

"Yeah, right."

"I'm serious, CJ."

"What? Do you think I'm, an idiot? You're in a race. Of course you want to win."

"Not if I'm determined to teach a certain brunette a much-deserved lesson."

Uh oh. "You can't be serious."

"Would I joke about something like this?"

He was known throughout the United States for his pranks, of course he would. "I don't believe you. I refuse to accept that you would bilk the charity you're racing for out of...how much difference is there between first and last?"

"Twenty grand."

She gaped, not even flinching when he started the truck, the sound rivaling that of a 747. "*Twenty grand?* Bryce that's a lot of money for those children to lose out on."

"Don't worry, I have every intention of making up the difference."

He'd *what?*

He would. He'd make up the difference.

And then the true ramification of what he was telling her sank in. She stiffened in her seat. "You mean to tell me, I've been sitting in this truck for two friggin' days, hypothetically to cover a race a lot of people expect you to win, only now you tell me you have no intention of doing so?"

"Yup. And when I lose I'm going to blame it all on you."

"You wouldn't dare."

"Wouldn't I?"

Yes, he would. He was really truly that angry about how she'd booted him from the room. She fumed for a long, silent moment. "If you do this, Bryce, then I'll tell the Associated Press, my editor at *DRIVE*, every member of the press that this race is fixed." She crossed her arms in front of her and gave him a "take that" look.

It didn't seem to faze him because he just smiled in an all too knowing way and said, "No you won't. If you do that then I won't make up the difference between first and last, and if I do that, then the children lose out."

She stared at him for a long, simmering moment. "You wouldn't do something so petty just so you could...could..."

"Boink you?"

"Try to teach me a lesson," she contradicted.

"Oh, yes, I would."

"No way," she squeaked.

He actually laughed aloud. "You know, CJ, even if you'd been sincere in blackmailing me, I still wouldn't change my mind about Devil's Bones. You see, it's time you realized that sometimes, *I* like to have the upper hand."

"So exactly how do you plan on losing this race without Harry finding out? By slashing the tires?" He couldn't possibly be serious, but CJ just couldn't leave the subject alone.

They'd been out on the road for a half-hour, her nails practically embedded in the roll cage as they negotiated a rough stretch of road that rivaled the L.A. freeways.

"No. I'm fresh out of knifes today. I thought we'd get lost instead," Bryce answered as he steered the truck between two cacti. "So I guess you'll get your way after all. You won't be forced to ride along with me all day."

"Lost? How in the heck are you going to convince him we're lost when this truck is equipped with GPS?"

"Easy. We really *are* going to get lost."

CJ gawked at him, then turned and stared out at the barren expanse around them, bits of scrub faced off with cactus like Wyatt Earp at the O.K. Corral, the huge cacti raising their arms as if in surrender. She sympathized with those cacti right now.

"You've got to lay off snorting that starter fluid, Bryce. It's affected the few brain cells you have left."

"Racers get lost out here all the time. Take the wrong fork and wham, you're off course. And GPS only tells you where you are, not how to get back home."

"You mean you don't have a TomTom or a Garmin or something?"

He shot her a glance meant to convey his amusement at the silliness of her question. "We have maps," he said. "Which I forgot to bring today."

Liar.

She would just bet he forgot. CJ released her death grip on the roll cage and murmured, "Amazing. Even with thousands of dollars worth of equipment, men *still* manage to get lost. And if there was a gas station around, you probably wouldn't stop to ask directions."

"Probably not. But if I see one I'll be sure to pull over."

She rolled her eyes. "And I still don't think Harry is stupid enough to believe you, nor that you're actually going to do this. I happen to know they can track people via GPS."

"Trust me, sweetheart, our GPS unit will be miles away from where we really are."

"What do you mean?"

"Darn thing fell off at the start of the race."

"It did not."

"I'm afraid so," he said with a false smile.

"Bastard."

"I only have your best interest at heart."

"Yeah, well, the last man who said that left me with ten thousand dollars worth of credit card bills."

"Jeez. What'd he buy you? A new car?"

"No. He bought himself a new motorcycle," she grumbled. At his raised brows she dared him to say something derogatory. He didn't, but that didn't reassure her. It'd been nearly an hour since she'd first climbed into the truck with him. That meant their first check point was up ahead. Would he let her out? And if he didn't, how would she escape?

And escape she would.

Bryce in a hotel room she could handle—well, once she got her wits about her—Bryce out in the middle of the desert with no distractions, no interruptions, no phone to dial 911 when she had her heart attack from his lovemaking was something she was determined to avoid at all cost, which meant she would have to fake an illness, ask Bryce to drop her off at the next stop. There was no way she could let him make love to her. Last night was close enough.

Last night had been heaven.

Yes, it had, but she wouldn't let him touch her again. He might be delusional about how she looked, but she wasn't delusional about how this would end. He would leave her high and dry once the race ended.

The radio crackled, Harry saying, "Ah, Bryce?" in a panicked tone. "We got a problem here. Would you do a position check for us?"

CJ's brows rose, confused by the odd request, but when she looked at Bryce she knew. A groan rose in her throat, a groan which grew louder when Bryce gave her a smile that could only be called Machiavellian. "Sure, Harry," he said.

She leaned her head back and closed her eyes, mumbling, "Bryce Danvers, don't you dare tell me you were serious about leaving that GPS behind."

She heard his naughty little chuckle, then the words that set her heart to beating like the drums in a reggae band. "Now, now, CJ, when have you ever known me to lie?"

Chapter Eleven

"You...you...you, putz!"

He quirked a brow at her saying, "I thought I was a bastard."

"Damn it, Bryce," Harry's frantic voice interrupted. "Boink her later. I need your position. *Now.*"

Bryce shot her an amused smile. "What should I tell him? Missionary? Doggie? What's your pleasure? Well, aside from sixty-nine. I know you like that. Or should I dub what I did to you thirty-four-and-a-half. What's half of sixty-nine?"

"Stop it, Bryce."

"Bryce?" Harry's voice boomed again.

"Roger, Harry," Bryce said, but he didn't even look down, just said, "Well, would you look at that. The display shows an error message."

"Sonofabitch, Bryce. That's what we thought. Your GPS isn't working."

"That's because he left it at the start/finish line," CJ yelled.

"Now, now, Ceej, don't be telling any lies," Bryce said with a smile bright enough to light up the dark side of the moon. She wished *he* was on the dark side of the moon.

"Bryce," Harry cried. "Did you copy?"

He looked away from her. "Roger, Harry. We copy. We'll pull

over and try to figure out where CJ went wrong." He took his foot off the gas.

CJ jerked in her seat. "Where I went wrong?" she snapped, watching as Bryce unplugged her mic. "*You're* the one who left the darn thing behind. Don't you dare tell him I got us lost just to suit your petty sense of revenge."

He chuckled. CJ balled her hands into fists, her anger gaining momentum in direct opposition to the speed of the truck. "Why the heck do we have to stop?"

The smile turned to a leer. "What's the matter, honey? You scared? You should know it'll be good. Even better than last night."

She clenched her hands in her lap. "The only thing I'm scared of is catching the clap from you."

"You don't have to worry about that," he said smugly. "I brought lots of condoms. Green ones, yellow ones. Ribbed, unribbed. Here." He reached behind the seat. "Choose."

CJ gaped at him in horror as he dumped a smorgasbord of safety on her lap, sunlight catching the foil packages and turning the inside of the truck into bright prisms of speckled color.

She stared down at them in disbelief. Her eyes narrowed in on a green and white package with the words, "Extra Large" emblazoned on the front. She looked at another one. They were all extra large. "Great," she muttered sarcastically. "Did you bring sunscreen too?"

He didn't hesitate a beat as he answered, "For my rear?"

"As in you being on top? I don't think so."

"But, I'm always on top."

"Not this time, bud. Not now, not ever. You can get rid of the condoms and the sunscreen." She shoved the foil packages off her lap, hearing them scatter on the sheet metal floor with a sense of satisfaction.

"You like making love *au natural*, eh?"

"The only thing you're going to make love to is the Joceline in a Box. So you can just drop the Casanova routine."

He laughed again as the truck finally came to a dust disturbing stop. CJ's heart beat even louder. The desert stretched for miles around them, the road was on a slight incline which dissolved ahead into small mountains, blue sky and fuzzy white clouds. CJ unclenched hands when she felt her fingernails digging furrows into her palm, then tensed again as Bryce cut the engine, the absolute quiet of desert so complete it was almost deafening.

The thump in her ears grew louder, her breath came faster. *This is ridiculous, CJ,* a little voice warned. *Get a hold of yourself.*

I'd rather get a hold of Bryce, the devil inside her answered back.

Well, you can't have him. He only wants you because you happen to be more convenient than the blow-up doll stashed behind the seat.

Who cares? answered that other voice. *He's the sexiest man you've ever laid eyes on. You'd give up chocolate for a year in order to have him. And if can make you scream like he did by just using his mouth, just imagine—*

"CJ?"

She jumped, the sound of his voice so near, for a moment she forgot she had a helmet on. But it was the way he put his hand on her leg that suddenly made her palms wet as hand wipes, made her legs tremble like a marathon runner, made her breath catch like a diver entering a pool of freezing water.

"CJ, it's time for us to pick up where we left off yesterday."

She leaned her head back, closed her eyes and groaned.

"C'mon, Ceej, there's nothing to be afraid of."

Just herself!

She heard him undo his harness, opening her eyes a crack to spy him taking off his helmet. Then came the distinct crackle of Velcro as he pulled apart his firesuit. Something about that sound sent her frayed nerves over the edge. Suddenly she wanted out of that truck. *Now!*

Her hands became a frenetic burst of energy as she fumbled with the straps on her helmet, undid the myriad of belts and buckles and jerked aside the safety harness.

"C'mon, honey, it's not *that* big," Bryce called as she hurled herself out the window like a paratrooper.

Yes, it was. She'd seen the size of it last night.

She landed on her hands and knees with a dust raising thud. A lizard dashed under a nearby rock. Must be one of Bryce's cousins.

She heard Bryce move and looked back. He was leaning out the passenger window, his eyes glinting with delighted humor. "Ohhh. *I* get it. Oh. So you *do* want it doggie style, huh?"

She was going to rip off the front bumper and brain him with it. She turned away, eyeing the rocky, barren terrain around her for any sign of snakes, scorpions or mutant jackrabbits before grimly striding back the way they had come.

"CJ, hon, keep a sharp ear out for the rattle."

She halted, so frustrated she was tempted to kick the rear tire. "Don't you call me your hon, you...you walking pile of testosterone. They should call you a *pubic* figure instead of a *public* figure."

Silence greeted her words. She turned on her heel, but she

hadn't even reached the end of the truck before she heard the distinct thud of feet landing behind her. How in the heck he managed to exit the truck so quickly was beyond her, but the next instant his hand closed around her elbow and she forgot everything save the fact that she wanted...no, desperately needed that hand to stroke her.

That terrified her even more.

"CJ, what is it?" His voice sounded different. Concerned. Confused.

She tilted her chin and tried to sound firm. "I'm leaving," she hissed.

"What do you mean 'you're leaving'?" He looked around him. "We're in the middle of the desert."

"Oh my gosh." She slapped her forehead with her palm "And I thought we were on the holo deck of the Starship Enterprise."

He stared down at her, his black brows slowly rising, the hot desert breeze ruffling his hair. "Very funny, but your sarcasm can't hide the fact that you're scared. You aren't really, are you? I mean after last night..."

Somehow she managed a look of disdain on her face. "Scared of you...hardly," with enough sincerity to sound marginally true.

He saw right through it. "Yes, you are, and now you're running away."

She crossed her arms in front of her. "I'm not running away. I'm...I'm taking a nature walk."

He snorted.

She glared.

"You're scared," he said with absolute certainty.

"No, I'm not." Not of him physically. Didn't he get that yet?

She was afraid of how he made her feel.

"Prove it."

"How?"

"Kiss me."

If it meant he'd leave her alone afterward, she'd do anything. "Fine." And with that she took a step toward him, observing with satisfaction as his eyes widened just before she pulled his head down and pressed her lips against his.

That was when it happened...and it was all his fault.

One minute she was CJ Randall, woman-teaching-man-a-lesson and the next she was CJ Randall, pushed-beyond-her-limit-nymphomaniac.

She lost it, lost complete control of her faculties. Her body seemed to know it was Bryce who was touching her. Bryce who had made her cry out in pleasure only hours before. Bryce who could do that to her again. She wanted him. Not in the way he'd taken her last night. She wanted him inside her. It didn't matter that they were out in the middle of the desert with an audience of insects and reptiles watching their every move. It didn't matter that she was lowering herself to the level of Pink Pumps. All that mattered was the here and now.

And she wanted him.

Here. Now.

She kissed him long and hard, feeling his hands clasp her waist. But that wasn't good enough. She jerked open his firesuit like some sex-crazed heroine in one of Harry's movies, the Velcro ripping apart with a soul-satisfying *riiiiiip* and when she found the hair on his chest, she ran her fingers through it, hearing him groan, a deep man-type groan that sent her hyperactive libido into slam bammin' overdrive. This time *she* would take the upper hand. This time *she* would bring him to a climax.

He was naked beneath that firesuit. Man-oh-man was he ever naked.

"Damn, CJ," he hissed against her lips, "I guess you're not as scared as I thought."

He tugged apart her firesuit. She helped him as she shrugged it from her body in a move that would have done a belly-dancer proud. Hot desert sun stung her shoulders, all that suddenly stood between them was a sleeveless tank top and a pair of very unflattering stretch pants. Oh, and two triangular spots of satin and an even smaller triangle that were her cotton panties. She didn't care...just flat out didn't give a dang, all she wanted was his glorious, *naked* body next to her overweight, *almost* naked body.

So when he tugged down her stretch pants, she didn't protest, was glad that he did. She didn't care that he jerked the tank top off her next. He made quick work of her undergarments too, until they were both buck naked in the middle of the desert. And when he suddenly pressed her against the tailgate of the truck, she didn't care about that, either. She *wanted* it rough, wished he would toss her over his shoulder and drag her off to the nearest cave.

His lips met hers, kissing her hard, kissing her lean, kissing her mean. Every nerve ending was on fire. Every brush of his skin nearly sent her to orgasm heaven.

Orgasm? Yet again, what was building inside of her didn't feel like a simple orgasm. It was like a nuclear explosion, especially with his hand creeping slowly toward her lips, and not the ones on her face.

"Oh man," she moaned when he touched her. It all came back. Every glorious thing he'd done to her last night. She wanted that again. Bad. "Yes," she breathed. It was incredible how all he had to do was touch her and she damn near fell apart—more than incredible—it was...it was...beyond words.

"CJ," he groaned.

"I know," she moaned back. Bryce shoved her firesuit beneath her butt before she burned, not that she'd have noticed. She was already on fire, what was happening between them unbelievable. Like being twisted and coiled into a knot.

He could feel it too, she could tell by the way his hand trembled as he touched her, tasted it on his lips which once again covered her own, heard it in the ragged edge of his breathing.

She clasped her hand around him. He tilted his head back and released a hiss of pure, masculine pleasure. And when she started stroking him in the same way he touched her she could feel his breath waft across her face and mingle with the dusty desert air.

"CJ, honey," he murmured, "I'm going to explode if you don't stop."

She paused for a heartbeat, then started raining kisses down his chest. "Go for it," she murmured back. She would join him. They could explode together. It could make the evening news, "Couple explodes in desert, details at ten o'clock."

She clasped her arms around his neck and lifted herself so that her legs wrapped around his waist. He stiffened in surprise. Her back bumped up against the tailgate again, but she was too intent on lowering herself onto him to care.

"Whoa, CJ," Bryce groaned. "What about protec—?"

She impaled herself. Felt him slide inside of her...filling her...stretching her. She moaned, or was that him? She didn't know, didn't care. Everything she'd ever fantasized about was happening, everything save one last detail. She opened her eyes. She needed to see him stare down at her as if she was the only woman in the world...pretend for just a moment that she mattered to him as much as he mattered to her.

Their gazes met. Her breath caught.

He looked at her like she was the center of his universe.

"CJ," he said tenderly. "Oh, CJ." He leaned down and kissed her with a tenderness that brought tears to her eyes. She forgot everything then, everything save the incredible feel of his tongue mimicking the rhythm of her hips. She rocked up and down on him, wanting it hard and fast, soft and slow, she wanted it all. And she wanted it *now*.

Her orgasm hit hard. It made her cry out in shock, in pleasure-pain, in wonder. It was so sudden and consumed her so totally, she barely noted Bryce's own cry. Her whole body clutched around his, absorbed him, opened to him, the beat of her body bursting into a million, jagged pieces.

The ground moved.

The world tilted.

The universe shattered.

And when she docked back at Earth, she arrived with a mighty big thump.

It took a while, but slowly she became aware of her surroundings.

That's when it hit her.

She'd just pumped a man like Annie Oakley on the way to the promise land.

Worse, she was still hanging onto that same man wearing nothing but her racing shoes and a pair of cotton undies slung around her left ankle. And her bra...her bra had landed on a nearby barrel cactus, the white triangles looking like cartoon eyes peering up at her from above a bra-strap smiley face.

She closed her eyes and groaned, "Oh, man," under her

breath.

Bryce stirred against her, his big hands clutching her more firmly against him, one thumb stroking her back in a lazy, circular motion. "I know, babe." He leaned back enough so that he could stroke a stray wisp of hair out of her face. "Incredible."

Babe? Had he just called her *babe*?

"If you wait a few minutes, we can do it again."

Her eyes snapped open at that, pushing on his shoulder so she could lean back. "I wouldn't bet on it."

"I would." He gave her that sexy look of his.

She wiggled in his arms, trying to get him to release her. Not a smart thing to do as it turned out, not given their, er, intimate connection.

"What're you doing?"

"I want to get dressed."

"Why?"

"I'm getting sunburned."

He bought it, his blue eyes searching her face intently before slowly letting her go. Heat pulsed through her at the feel of him gliding from her body. She ignored it, and when her feet touched the wobbly ground, she unsteadily stepped away and pulled up her undies. Her clothes lay on the bumper, looking as empty and uncomfortable as she felt. She picked them up, shook the dust off and jerked on her pants and tank top. Her firesuit followed.

"CJ, is something wrong?"

He sounded concerned, and for some reason that irked her all the more, probably because he was still stark naked, leaning against the truck, his firesuit wadded up around his ankles like one of those flasher dolls she'd seen at a joke store. And that reminded her of who Bryce Danvers was: America's Playboy

Prankster. A man who had more money than the Shah of Iran. Well, maybe not that much, but there was no way he could possibly still be interested in her. He'd want to move onto greener pastures now that he'd had her—just like Ed.

"If it's something I've done, just tell me."

"All right. You want to know? I'll tell you. I just had sex with a man who's dipped his wick into more wax pots than a candle maker."

His eyes narrowed. "Is that why you look so upset?" he asked, hands on his very naked hips. "Are you jealous of my past relationships?"

"Relationships? Is that what they call one-night stands these days?"

"No."

"How about quickies?"

"CJ, really." His expression softened. "Is that all you're worried about?"

She didn't say anything. Let him think what he wanted.

"Look, if it makes you feel any better, I have myself checked regularly."

She snorted. "I'm not surprised. They probably have a Baccarat crystal vial at the hospital with your name permanently etched on it. No doubt you're on a first name basis with all the nurses too."

"Only the good looking ones," he beamed.

"So you do have your standards...amazing. I rest my case."

"You *are* jealous."

"Only of the fact that those nurses got to poke you with sharp instruments and I don't."

"I don't get it." He sounded exasperated, his expression

growing more and more confused. "You're so worked up. What'd I do?"

She was about to tell him he'd just boinked her for the first and last time when she heard a distant whump—whump—whump. She tilted her head, her eyes searching the horizon for the source of the sound.

It was a helicopter, heading straight toward them, the blue and white logo emblazoned on the front clearly discernible even from this angle.

"Damn," Bryce swore.

She turned toward him. He reached down to pull up his firesuit.

"Hurry," she urged, making sure her own firesuit was fastened securely.

"I'm trying."

He wrestled with it some more, but the firesuit was firmly entangled around his ankles. When he looked up at her, CJ knew they were in trouble.

The helicopter drew close enough to see three figures inside, one of them pointing a TV camera right at them. She stared up at it for a second, the whump-whump-whumps getting louder and louder.

"Why me?" she moaned when she recognized the situation was hopeless.

Bryce didn't help matters any when he calmly said from behind her, "Now *this* is what I call national exposure."

Chapter Twelve

"You're not still mad at me, are you, hon?" Bryce asked a half hour later, glancing at CJ as he did so. He was heartily sick of the silence in the truck, silence but for the usual ping of rocks, the roar of the engine, and the clink and clatter of the racing chassis as they rumbled through a small canyon, beams of light flickering in and out of the cabin. He was going to miss this old truck when the race was over.

"CJ?" He reached out and touched her leg, glancing into the rear view mirror and at the stream of dust trailing behind like a transparent parachute.

She jumped like a startled jackalope, snapping, "Don't touch me."

Yup. Still mad. Either that or she had a helluva case of PMS. Again. "What's wrong? Shoulders hurting you some?"

Out of the corner of his eye he saw her glance at him and for some reason it made him tense.

"My shoulders aren't the problem."

"Then what is it?" he asked for about the tenth time, although not really expecting an answer. She'd been strangely silent since they'd climbed in the car.

"I just got caught on national television with a naked man standing next to me and you're wondering what's *wrong*?" She kicked at the foil packets littering the floor.

He *could* point out that she was who the one who had undressed *him*, but he didn't think that was wise. She looked ready to pop a gasket. "C'mon, Ceej," he said soothingly instead. "It's not that bad. I doubt they'll really use the footage. And if they do, black bars will cover the worst of it."

Silence greeted his words, and when he looked over at her he could tell that probably wasn't the smartest thing to say. Maybe it would help if he told her that making love to her on the back of his truck had been the best sex he'd had in a long, long time...maybe ever. Nah, she'd probably take it wrong. Besides, she was so damn cute when she was mad. It was one of the things he liked about her. One of the many things, he amended. Every day she surprised him anew. Today it'd been her response to his lovemaking. He'd suspected she'd be a firecracker in the lovemaking department, and she was.

"You're right," she snapped. "*They* probably won't use it. They'll sell it to the Tattler instead."

"Yeah, but look at the bright side. They could have filmed you jumping me."

Her head snapped toward him like a rabid dog. "I did *not* jump you."

"Like Roy Rogers hopping on Trigger," he contradicted.

"*You* were the one who slammed me against the truck like a Neanderthal."

"And you loved every minute of it."

"Don't delude yourself."

"If that was delusion, I'd like to get deluded more often."

She turned to glare at him. "Is sex all you think about?"

"No. I've been thinking about *you* for three days." He kept his eyes steady ahead.

"You need help."

"No, I need *you.*"

"At least until the next woman comes along," she muttered.

He stared at her in disbelief. "Is that what you think? That all I want from you is sex?"

"You're a man, of course that's all you want."

He could think of nothing to say, at least not at first. "Did it ever cross your mind that I might want to be with you because I think you're special?"

"Ha."

"You are."

"Right. And just like Ed, you'll use me and lose me."

He slammed on the brakes, the truck skidding and sliding to a bone-jarring, body-slamming halt.

"Hey," CJ yelled as she clutched at the roll cage with both hands.

Her shoulders. Damn. "Sorry," he said.

"I'm not going to have any skin left," she mumbled.

He felt bad about that, but damn it, he wasn't going to let that comment about Ed slip. Dust rose around them like steam from a volcanic fissure, bits of gravel pinged off the underside. He turned to face her.

She stared at him with wide, green eyes. "I mean, really, Bryce, if you had to go to the bathroom, there's easier ways to slow down."

"You're comparing me to Ed?" He shook his head in disgust. "So the bastard broke up with you, that's no reason to—"

"*He* didn't break up with me, *I* broke up with him once I realized what he was truly after."

"A new motorcycle?" he guessed.

"No," she said. "Ed wasn't the one who bilked me out of ten-thousand dollars. Ed was the man who cost me my last job."

Wow. And he thought he had some bad taste. "What happened?"

She shook her head, almost as if she wasn't going to answer. "He raided my idea file."

"Excuse me?"

She met his gaze. "My idea file. For articles. I had no idea he'd taken a peek at it until the first of my ideas ended up as front page news, under *his* byline. When I confronted him about it, he made it sound as if I was crazy. But then he did it again and I got angry. Unfortunately, the senior editor believed him over me."

"That's not fair."

"*Life* isn't fair," she said.

"And now you think *I'm* using you, too?" It all clicked into place. At last he understood. But *this* he could deal with.

She glanced at him. "Shouldn't I? You're never with one woman for very long. And every picture I've ever seen of you you've always had a woman by your side who looked like Cinderella with a boob job and on a good hair day. How can I hope to compete? Not that I want to, mind you," she added quickly.

"You want to, all right."

"Hah."

"And all those other women meant nothing to me."

"Just like I won't mean anything when having sex with Blimpo the Hippo wears off, trust me."

"Your self-image is so way off, CJ. Don't you ever look in

the mirror?"

"Yeah, it cracks every time."

"Bull. You have a beautiful body, and the most gorgeous pair of eyes I've ever seen. And, obviously, I'm not the only one who thinks so. Or did you forget Miles, the boss that made a pass at you too?"

"Oh, I remember."

"Then you should recognize how beautiful you are."

"Oh yeah?" she asked, looking out the window again. *Ed told me the same thing.* The words were unspoken, but he knew she was thinking them. Damn it. Didn't she know that he was nothing like Ed? Didn't she understand she had more going for her than looks? There were streaks of dirt and grime on her face. Her dark, chestnut hair peeked out from beneath the helmet in static spikes. A sheen of moisture covered her upper lip, but to him she was the most beautiful creature he'd ever seen.

And it hit him in that instant that he'd really fallen for her.

"*Bryce,*" Harry's voice bellowed over the radio. "*I hope you're not off course again.*"

Bryce didn't answer for a moment, but when CJ remained obstinately silent, he clicked open the mic. "We're fine, Harry."

"*Good. 'Cause I'm hoping you and CJ are planning to finish the race sometime today? Or should I call up the Children's Foundation and give them your credit card number instead?*"

"Just give us a second," Bryce said, the amazing revelation he'd had making him struggle for thought. *He really, really liked her.*

Silence, then a brief burst of static. "*What? You and CJ trying to flash more helicopters?*"

CJ jerked in her seat.

"No, Harry. We just needed to make a little pit stop."

"How'd he find out about the helicopter?" CJ whispered frantically.

"Ahh, Harry. CJ wants to know how you heard about the helicopter?"

"*Heard about it? Hell. Who hasn't?*"

CJ leaned back in her seat and groaned.

"Roger, Harry. Thanks, we'll be on our way in a sec."

"I'm dead," CJ moaned. "The minute I get back to the office I'm dead."

"Relax, hon."

"*Relax.* I'm about to lose my job, my reputation is going to be in shreds, and you want me to relax?" She glared over at him. "Thanks. I'll try to remember that when I'm standing in the unemployment line, or when I'm living in a cardboard box because I couldn't afford to pay my rent."

She'd never come near a cardboard box, not if he had anything to say about it. Now that some of the shock of his revelation had worn off, he realized how right it all was. CJ might take a little convincing, but one day she would know it too. All she needed was to accept that she wasn't a flash in his pants.

"You're not going to lose your job," he said gently.

"Oh, yeah? That's what you think."

"Why would Miles fire you over this? You didn't do anything wrong."

"You don't understand. Miles hates me. I rejected him, remember?"

"Of course I remember, but he wouldn't take it that far, would he? He wouldn't really fire you for getting involved with me, would he?"

For a long moment CJ debated whether or not to tell him. But what the heck. Maybe she could scare him off. "Actually, there's more to the story than I told you before."

He stared across at her with lifted brows. As if to ask, *yeah, so?*

"When he was out of the office one day, I squeezed Crazy Glue into his condoms."

"Excuse me?"

"I knew he carried them because he had one out that day in the closet."

"You're kidding."

"Nope. Bastard carries them around in the event he can corner some other hapless female in a supply closet. So I squeezed Crazy Glue into his condoms then re-sealed the packages. I thought it would harden the darn things up, you know, sort of spoil his moment of passion, but damned if that glue stayed moist."

His mouth dropped open.

"Not only that, but from what I heard, he was able to pull the thing on. Glued the latex right to him."

His eyes widened.

"The paramedics had to use acetone to get it off. Which was the only thing Miles got off on for the next two months. I guess it took a while for the skin to heal."

She settled back in her seat and waited for his reaction.

It came almost immediately.

He threw back his head and laughed, roared so hard CJ almost jerked the helmet from her head to stop it from resonating in her ears.

"Damn," he gasped. "That has to be the best revenge story I've ever heard."

"I'm almost positive he knows it was me, but he can't prove it. So he amuses himself by sending me on the most miserable of assignments, and making my life hell, and doing whatever else he can to exact revenge."

He was grinning from ear-to-ear. "Sounds like Miles is a real schmuck with no sense of humor."

"Would you think it funny if someone glued your hand to, well, you know where?"

"It depends on who did the gluing and if whipped cream was involved."

"You're sick."

"C'mon, Ceej, you sound like you actually feel sorry for the guy."

"Feel sorry for Miles? Hah! I only wish his other hand had been glued to his behind."

"Then what's wrong?"

She looked away from him. "Nothing. Everything."

"You're worried I'm going to dump you, too, aren't you?"

Duh! Hadn't she come right out and admitted that fifteen minutes ago? "How can I be worried over something that will never happen?"

"You're right, CJ It will *never* happen." And danged if he didn't look at her with the tenderness of a lover, which he was...had been. Once. Never again.

"You misunderstand me, Bryce. It's not going to happen because *you* and *I* aren't going to happen."

"CJ—"

"When we arrive at the next checkpoint, I'm getting out," she continued, "you and I will go our separate ways. No hard feelings."

"No hard feelings," he repeated incredulously.

"Yes. I want to end it here. It was fun, but—"

"—why don't you give me a call sometime," he finished for her through his teeth. "Is that what you were going to say?"

"Actually, I was about to suggest we be friends."

His black brows rose. "C'mon, Ceej. There's more to our relationship than that."

Yes. Yes, there was. For her. And that scared the bejeezus out of her. So she was pulling the plug. Now. Before things got too out of hand and she opened herself up to even more hurt.

"Besides," he continued, the look in his eyes one she'd never seen before. "I told you I'm not stopping to let you out today."

"Bryce—"

"It's just a few more hours, CJ. You're not going to give up so easily, are you?"

"I have no choice."

"Sure you do. Just sit back. Enjoy the ride. I promise to take care of you. No more bruises. Think about things for a little while. Think about *us*."

"You're not going to give up, are you?"

"CJ, honey, I haven't gotten where I am today by stepping back and allowing something I want to slip through my fingers."

Determination. That's what was in his eyes. Hard, steely determination. Gone was Bryce-the-carefree-playboy, in his place was Bryce-the-hot-blooded-predatory-male.

"And, CJ, I want you."

Heaven help her, his words sent a pulse of liquid lust surging through her veins.

So she stuck it out, but the second the race was over she did what any self-respecting female in her position would do. She ignored the call of the wild and ran for the hills, slinking around the truck stop parking lot the officials had commandeered for the end of the race like Bugs Bunny avoiding Elmer Fudd. It was actually pretty easy. The parking lot was jammed with people. The haulers were parked in a long line leading right up to front door of the diner. For a moment CJ contemplated hiding inside the beige building, but that was too obvious. No. Best to wait somewhere else, somewhere where Bryce would never think of looking. She straightened suddenly.

One of the haulers.

Specifically, Kathleen Seavers's hauler. Bryce would never think of looking for her there.

She turned away, making her way through the crowd and grumbling under her breath the whole way. It was packed. Apparently half of Nevada had wanted to watch the end of the race. Well, at least there was one thing to be grateful for. The race was over.

"CJ," a little voice called out excitedly.

CJ turned, spying one of the little boys she'd met at the beginning of the race. Daniel.

"Hey, kiddo," she called in greeting. "What are you doing here?"

"Susan brought me over. She's over there," he motioned to somewhere behind him. She spotted the woman trying to make her way through a crowd, a harried expression on her face. "I wanted to be at the finish line when Bryce crossed it, but we were late. Did he win?"

"No," she said. "I'm sorry, kiddo, but we, ah, we broke down out there."

"Aww, too bad," he said.

He looked so disappointed she found herself squatting down next to him and saying, "Hey. Maybe he'll make it up to you. Maybe he'll take you shopping in one of his stores or something."

"You think?" the kid asked, his face lighting up. But then his smile faded. "He already does so much for of us. Did you know he bought us a new home?"

That caught CJ's attention. "He did what?'

Daniel was nodding, his face full of pride as he explained, "It wasn't really new. The home we were living in was falling apart. Mr. Danvers had some men come in and fix it. Paid for a hotel for us to stay in while they worked on it and everything. It was neat. I got to swim at the hotel every day."

She huffed out a breath of disbelief. Okay, maybe not disbelief, more like resignation.

"That's neat," she said, glancing around, terrified she'd see Bryce. It couldn't take him that long to say a few words into a camera.

"Listen, Daniel. I'll speak to Bryce personally about that shopping trip, just the minute I see him."

"Do you know where he is?" Daniel asked.

"He's over by the finish line," she said, pointing back the direction she'd come. "And I'm sure he'd love to see you."

"Okay, thanks," and the kid was off like a shot, Susan darting past CJ in hot pursuit, a hastily muttered greeting aimed her way. She really was glad the race was over, she told herself, spotting the Snappy Lube hauler up ahead. Her shoulders were killing her and she doubted she'd be able to sit down without wincing for a week. Once she found Kathleen, she could bum a ride to her hotel and get out of Dodge.

If you're so glad, why do you feel so downright depressed?

Because I'm about to start my period, she screamed at the voice. *Now leave me alone while I try to escape.*

She found the Seavers' transporter parked four spaces away, a crowd clustered around the open back as they waited for the off-road racing legend to make an appearance. CJ fought her way through them and flagged down the nearest person wearing a Snappy Lube uniform; an older man with thin, gray hair and skin gone craggy from too many hours in the sun.

"Is Kathleen Seavers around?" she asked, wondering if he'd ever thought of using a moisturizer.

"She's inside the helicopter...I mean the hauler."

She was so intent on studying his skin that at first his words didn't register, then her eyes narrowed. Good Lord. Did everybody know about the helicopter?

"Very funny," she muttered.

"Go on in," the man said.

She did exactly that.

There was just one problem.

Bryce was sitting in the lounge when she opened the door.

Damn. Damn. And double damn. If it weren't for Kathleen's presence, she would've stomped her feet in frustration.

"There she is," he cried like a man greeting a long, lost relative. "CJ, we were just talking about you."

She placed her hands on her hips and glared. "I thought you were giving interviews."

He smiled complacently. "And I thought *you* were in the bathroom."

"I *was* in the bathroom," she lied. "The one in the restaurant."

"Ah huh," he drawled in his southern accent.

"I was."

"Sure, CJ, and I'm Dwight Yokum."

"Yeah, well I hated your last album."

His smile grew.

So did her ire. "Damn it, Bryce, can't a girl have some time alone? I was hoping Kathleen and I could, er, chat." Which was probably sounded stupid, but it was worth a try.

"Later," he clipped, his blue eyes swinging toward his friend's wife. "Kathleen, darlin', would you mind leaving us alone for a minute?"

To her credit, Kathleen looked uncomfortable with the request. Perhaps she was feeling bad about the hotel room incident. "Well, I ah—

"Lock it too, will you, Kath?"

"No," CJ said. "Don't go."

Clearly the woman was torn, but her loyalty to Bryce won out. That or she worried about losing her husband's new sponsorship deal.

"You and I can talk later," she said, slipping out the door before CJ could call her back. The key clicked in the lock. CJ squelched the urge to fly after her. Instead she kept her eyes firmly focused on Bryce, a Bryce who looked like Hollywood's version of a race car driver with his slight shadow of stubble on his chin, his skin tanned from the desert sun, and his blue eyes sparkled with mischief and something else.

"CJ," he said with a wolfish smile. "Why don't you come on over and sit down next to me."

"Not without a can of Raid."

She caught the smile which just about broke free before he shook his head. "And there you go being rude to me again."

"Get used to it because that's all you'll ever get from me."

"Oh, I'm used to it all right. Hell, I kinda like it."

"I'm not surprised. You probably like whips and chains too."

He pursed his lips, a look of mock consideration on his face. "Nope. But with you I might be willing to give it a try."

"Great. I'll talk to Harry about getting you some. He might even be able to arrange someone to play with you too."

He smiled, a donkey-in-the-grain-bin sort of smile. "But I don't want to play with someone else. I want to play with *you*."

"Don't bet the farm on it, Bryce."

He shifted then slowly unfurled himself from the couch. "Oh, I'd be willing to bet a lot more than the farm, CJ."

CJ resisted the urge to step back. The Seavers' lounge was an exact duplicate of Harry's except for the small desk to her left. Unfortunately, that meant throwing herself out the window was out of the question. There *was* no window. She crossed her arms in front of her chest and said, "You'd lose."

"Lose what?"

"Your bet."

"Would I?"

She tilted her chin. "Absolutely."

"Care to test that theory?"

She uncrossed her arms. "And how exactly do you plan on doing that?" she asked bravely, too bad it was such a stupid question. She could see *exactly* how he planned on doing it.

"Stick around and you'll find out."

She *wanted* to be stuck all right, which just proved her theory. She was a masochist. A part of her didn't care that he had the power to hurt her thousand times more than Ed ever had. And that thought scared her too. But she still couldn't help but wonder if it'd feel any better on a couch than on the bumper of a truck, not that she could let that happen.

"Nope. No way," she said aloud in an attempt to convince herself.

"*Yes.* Yes, way, CJ." He took another step toward her. "You want it."

She told her feet to stay planted right where they were, even though they didn't want to listen to her. "No, I don't want it, Bryce."

He took another step, their bodies only inches apart now. "Yes, you do. You crave me, just the way I crave you."

She flicked her head. "What I'm craving is a Big Mac with cheese and a bag of fries all to myself."

"Liar," he said softly, taking another itty bitty step.

Her eyes caught on his lips. Such fine lips they were; well defined, masculine..."Sexy, er, ahh, I mean sex." She blinked up at him. "I meant to say there you go thinking about sex again."

"What I'm thinking about is *you*."

"Same thing."

"You're right."

She could feel his breath on her face. Her eyes caught on his lips again. Her whole body flared with heat. *Once. Just once more*, taunted that little voice. "No."

"No, what?"

"No, I'm absolutely not going to let this happen."

"That's too bad."

She looked up at him.

"Because I've every intention of *making* it happen, CJ."

Her heart skittered in her chest.

He stared down at her, his blue eyes so dark they looked

black. She let herself drift in that gaze for a moment.

"So if you want to leave, CJ, I suggest you do it now. The door doesn't lock from that side."

It didn't? Oh.

His head began to lower...slowly, oh so slowly. He was giving her time, time to slink away like a chastened puppy. But that hitherto unknown masochistic side promptly refused to budge. It also made her close her eyes, close her eyes and wait for a kiss that never came.

She peeked through her lashes. His head was still there, he was still staring down at her. She closed her eyes again.

Still nothing.

Her eyes popped open. "Have I got a booger hanging off the end of my nose or something?"

He smiled, that smug smile that made her toes curl. "No, I just wanted you to admit that you want me to kiss you."

He must have seen the answer in her face because he smiled, just before jerking her toward him. Their bodies connected; she gasped, a gasp which quickly died as his lips covered hers. He was right, she realized distantly. God, how he was right. She craved his kiss like a dog craved people food.

His hands found the Velcro opening of her firesuit, pulling it apart with a slow, tantalizing thoroughness that mimicked the job he was doing with that tongue of his. Dang. No wonder men loved their firesuits. Zap, and you were nearly naked. He just about drove her over the edge, especially when he somehow managed to peel her firesuit away in the world's fastest strip job. Not that she minded.

"You're not wearing a bra," he groaned against her lips.

She'd never put it back on, the fabric having been filled with cactus spines, but she didn't tell him that, couldn't have spoken if she'd wanted to because in the next instant he'd pulled her tank top away, his lips clamping on a nipple just before he suckled one to a hard point.

She moaned, tilting her head back and staring up at the ceiling. A hand brushed her side, then gently rolled down her stretch pants and undies all in one move. She let him, stepping out of everything all at the same time.

"Undress me," he murmured trailing kisses toward her collar bone.

If he'd told her to light her hair on fire she would have. At that moment she would have done anything for him, even danced naked wearing nothing but a glove on her head. So she stepped back and tugged at the Velcro of his firesuit, pulling the suit down to expose first his shoulders, then his darkly matted chest. When she reached his hips she hesitated a moment. He was hard for her, she could see that...Helen Keller could see that.

"Take it off."

She pulled the suit down lower until at last he was exposed. She closed her eyes and let him stroke her, wrapping her arms around his waist, content just to let him hold her. Then suddenly her skin began to tingle. Her body hummed.

She nuzzled his chest, inhaling his musky odor. He smelled like one of those pine-shaped car deodorants. She loved it, loved the way his hairy chest tickled her nose and made her want to sneeze. She found the tip of his nipple, he groaned when she lightly nipped him, then licked a circle around it.

"Damn, CJ, you could make the Tin Man cry with that tongue of yours."

She leaned back, looking into his blue, blue eyes, surrendering to the magic in them. "Kiss me, Bryce."

He didn't need to be asked twice.

He tasted sweet, like he'd been nibbling on the lime jelly beans she'd spotted on the desk. He angled his head to deepen the kiss.

She let her hands explore the contours of his back, let her body drift even closer.

He pressed her toward the couch, following her down, his hands caressing her breast in slow, sinuous patterns, and still he teased her lips with his own. His tongue brought her alive in a way she'd never dreamed of.

When she drew back, their lips hovered an inch apart.

"CJ," he whispered, his breath wafting over her face. He nuzzled her nose with his, then her cheek, his blue eyes staring into hers with a kind of wonderment. "Do you know what you do to me?"

She could feel what she did to him pressing against her left thigh. "I'd have to've been born without any nerve endings not to feel what I do to you."

He smiled, that sexy mouth of his dipping closer, "Let me *show* you what you do to me."

He shifted, his body fully covering hers. CJ closed her eyes and sighed. Her right leg dropped off the edge of the couch. His hand drifted to her side, then her hip, hovering over that part of her which craved his touch most. She arched toward him, pleading without words for his caress. He gave it to her, oh boy did he give it to her. Those magic fingers of his stroked, then fondled, then slowly delved deep inside her. She just about blew a fuse.

"Bryce, please."

She wanted more; she wanted all of him.

He must have understood because he shifted and then she could feel the pulsing heat of him at her opening.

"Yes," she cried as he sank partially into her. She cried out again. And yet, still, she wanted more...wanted all of him. Her hands dug into his shoulder blades. She pressed closer, squeezed harder, demanding that he give her everything and more. He slid in only a little deeper.

Not deep enough.

"Bryce," she cried out in frustration. Her short nails dug into his back.

"Hold on, CJ."

"I don't want to hold on."

He chuckled, a gentle puff of laughter that drifted across her sensitized skin. He nuzzled her neck, his mouth trailing a path back to hers. "Patience," he whispered.

Slowly, he sank into her another millimeter, then withdrew before sinking another millimeter. "Bryce," she warned. He was tormenting her. The schmuck.

He kissed her, cutting off her words and for a moment she was content to let their breaths mingle as one, to lap at the moist sweetness of his mouth. Then he moved against her and the ache between her legs turned into full-blown need.

"Is this what you want?" he whispered as he buried himself to the hilt.

"Yes," she cried out. "Oh yes."

"How's this?" he asked, withdrawing, then plunging back in.

"Better."

"And this?"

"Get...getting warmer."

"What about this?"

Her head thunked against the wall. "You're

getting...warmer."

She hardly noticed. Her brains were splattered like an upside down pizza. She braced her hands against the wall for the next one. "Ahh, now you're hot."

He found a rhythm, rocking in and out of her again and again. She locked her ankles around him and cried out.

Hard and fast.

Hot and wild.

She opened. He gave.

Harder and harder he thrust, her cries matching their rhythm. A pressure began to build and build and build. She shuddered, and then suddenly her whole body rocked with an orgasm. Hell, the whole transporter rocked. People in the next hauler probably rocked.

"CJ," Bryce gasped as he gained his own release.

"I know. I know," she panted with him.

For a long time they just held each other. She could feel the frantic beat of his heart against her pancaked breasts. Slowly her breathing returned to normal, but it was Bryce who spoke first.

"Wow," was all he said.

That summed it up.

Wow.

Double wow.

Double damn wow. His tongue stroked the shell of her ear. Her body goose pimpled in response. "I can't wait to make love to you in a bed."

"A bed. What's that?"

He chuckled, whispering, "You'll find out."

Would she? Was there a future for them? Deanna's words

rang in her ear. *Just go for it, Ceej.*

But she didn't know if she could. The sad truth was when it came right down to it she was a coward. A pure, unadulterated, lily-livered coward. Sure the sex was great...all right, better than great. But that's all it was: sex. She just didn't know if she could trust him not to hurt her. *Come on, Ceej, be honest. You're deathly afraid once the sex haze wears off he'll see you as you really are; plain, overweight CJ Randall.*

He shifted. "We should be leaving."

She didn't want to leave, didn't want reality to intrude. She wanted to stay with him all day and have hot, wild sex.

"Oh, so now that you've gotten what you want it's sayonara, baby?" she murmured half-jokingly, half serious.

He laughed. "No."

Man, she loved that laugh. Loved the way his eyes crinkled at the corner. Loved the way his whole face seemed to light up.

She could *so* easily fall in love with him.

CJ flinched, almost as if the realization had come out of nowhere and smacked her in the head. Abruptly, she stiffened.

"CJ, what is it?"

She pulled out of his arms, swiveling to sit on the edge of the couch. Oh, man, no.

"CJ?" he said, sitting up next to her.

No. No. No. No. No.

"What's wrong?"

She wanted to fall in love with him. To dive in with both feet. To sink beneath the surface...even if it meant drowning at the end.

"Honey, you're scaring me."

She looked at him and just about keeled over in terror.

"It's, ahh, nothing. Just a pain in my, err, my, ahh, foot."

"Your, err, ahh foot?"

She nodded. Her world felt as if it'd suddenly flipped upside down. What an idiot. How could she have allowed herself to dream, even to think for one moment that things could get serious between them? *Easy*, mused that little voice inside her head. *You never stood a chance.*

"Want me to rub it for you?" he asked, concern in his eyes.

No, she couldn't let him touch her. If she did she might grab him by the gonads and convince him to rub something else. She shivered and got up, pretending to limp as she picked up her firesuit. The air-conditioning in the transporter suddenly kicked on, the perfect excuse to pull on her clothes. "I'm fine, Bryce. It must have been a cramp, but it's, ahh, it's gone now."

Escape. She needed to escape.

"Are you sure you should be standing on it?" he asked as he pulled on his own clothes.

She looked at him.

And just about ran from the room right then. Oh, heavens, he looked so handsome. So concerned. So damn lovable.

"CJ?"

"I think I need to walk on it." She pushed on her shoes, ran a hand through her tangled hair and turned for the door.

"CJ, don't go yet. We need to talk."

About what? About which condo he'd set her up in? No, thank you.

"We'll talk later," she said in dismissal, checking to make sure he was dressed before opening the door.

Two of Nick's crew members stood at the bottom of the stairs.

CJ stared at them, aghast, all sorts of emotions surging through her. Embarrassment. Anger, and a sudden desperate need to be in Kansas. Had they been listening at the door? Yes. Yes, they had. She could tell by the smirks on their faces.

It seemed as if an oven door had been left open, her face burned so hot. One of the men was the same man who'd made the helicopter jibe. Without another word she pushed past them and exited the transporter like a woman whose pink pumps were on fire.

Chapter Thirteen

"And so what happened next?" Deanna asked the following Monday morning.

They were sitting in CJ's office, the glass windows behind her desk nearly blinding her after her attempt at drowning herself in a jug of margarita mix the night before. She had a headache, a brain-pounding, mind-numbing headache. Even her teeth throbbed.

"CJ?" Deanna asked, the brown eyes that matched her ebony skin staring at her in curiosity...and concern.

She looked up, the movement causing a sharp stab of pain to lance through her head. The black woman's face was filled with concern, her shoulder-length dark hair pulled back. "I just left, Deanna...ran away...hit the high road...hasta la vista, bab—"

"I get the picture," Deanna interrupted, holding up her hand. "Jeez, girl, I can't believe you did that."

"Believe it," CJ said, resting her forehead on her arms and sending a piece of paper flying off her desk and onto the carpet.

"But why? You had it goin' with one of America's top ten hunks. I can't believe you messed it all up like that."

"Yeah, well, believe it." CJ peeked up from her arms, blowing a hank of hair out of her eyes.

Deanna frowned. "You should call him."

"No way. I got out while there was still an outside chance I'd survive."

"That's why your eyes are all puffy like you've been crying?"

"Crying?" CJ asked, straightening and leaning back in her chair. "I haven't been crying."

All right, so maybe she'd cried a little, but only because she knew she was dreaming if she thought Bryce could be serious about a woman like her. And maybe she'd been a little upset because she just knew Miles was going to fire her. And when Saturday had blended into Sunday and Bryce hadn't called, she'd cried a little more. Sure she hadn't given him her phone number, but he could get it somehow. He could've, but he hadn't. So it was a good thing she'd left when she had. This way her heart didn't get broken. Not completely anyway.

Already is, Ceej, murmured that little voice. Because the truth of the matter was, she might have let herself care for Bryce a little more than she'd originally thought.

"Shut up," she told it right back.

"Don't tell me to shut up, girl. I'm just trying to warn you."

CJ refocused on her friend. "Huh?"

"I said, Miles is here, and he's got that smug little smile on his face. God, I hate that damned smile." Deanna stared out the window behind CJ's desk overlooking the parking lot. "Maybe you're right about getting fired, 'cause I doubt the man got laid, and I can't think of another reason for him to be grinnin' like that."

CJ groaned. Miles here? Before nine? Amazing. She straightened in her chair and swiveled around. Sure enough, there he was. Her lip curled. It was simply not fair that men grew more handsome as they got older. Miles managed to look the quintessential yuppie with his frosted blond hair, gray Versace suit (with a pink silk shirt beneath, no less), and Prada shoes. He stepped away from his cherry red BMW, clicked the arming button on his alarm, and headed for the entrance of the building. She turned back to Deanna.

"I guess it's time to beard the lion in his den," her friend said.

"Yeah, I suppose so."

"Buck up, kid. Maybe you'll get to tell Miles to piss off." With an encouraging smile, Deanna turned and left.

CJ watched her go. She would miss working with Deanna. Maybe she could convince her to quit too. Maybe they could both have a career in food services.

"Celia," Miles barked through her intercom five minutes later. "In my office. Now."

CJ stared at the intercom, "In my office now," she mimicked his words. She gritted her teeth. Despite facing a future of poverty, she heartily looked forward to *not* having to put up with any more of Miles's bull.

Squaring her shoulders she headed toward the worm's office, aware every eye was on her when she entered the common area.

"Close the door," Miles snapped when she entered the shrine to his journalistic accomplishments, most of which he'd swiped from other people.

She glanced around, trying to hide her revulsion as she eyed the wall of certificates on her left. That in itself wouldn't be so bad except he'd also erected shelves to her right; on those stood crystal phallic symbols—awards he'd garnered over the years—as well as framed magazine covers for all the publications he'd worked for. It was pretension at its worse.

"Good morning to you too, Miles."

He stood behind the tennis-court-sized desk, flipping through his mail and ignoring her. She recognized the ploy. He'd used it on more than one occasion. It wouldn't work. She took the opportunity to study him.

She supposed he'd had every reason to think she'd welcome his advances. She knew other women in the office did. It wasn't fair. Women aged like grapes, getting all dried up and shriveled after they put on forty pounds. Men aged like wine; getting better and better.

"Sit down," he finally deigned to say. "Or are you afraid that skirt of yours might split?"

He was referring to the black mini-skirt she'd bought this weekend in a fit of depression. Personally she'd thought the garment combined with her double-breasted, black jacket, and white silk blouse looked kind of cute. Leave it to Miles to say something snide.

And for the first time since going to work for him, CJ felt confident enough to say what she thought. Why not? It appeared she was about to get fired, anyway. "I wouldn't worry, Miles. If something splits, the thong I'm wearing covers the important parts."

His lip curled. "Thanks for sharing."

"Just thought you'd like to know. By the way, from the...ah, *looks* of things, I bet you're able to wear a postage stamp to cover *your* private parts."

His eyes narrowed. "Still trying to lose that twenty pounds, Celia?"

"At least I'm not afraid of Crazy Glue."

Direct hit. He stiffened, his hands clenching around his mail. "How'd you hear about that?"

She shrugged. "Who in this office hasn't?"

That was news to him. She could tell by the way he held himself erect. It took him a moment to regain his composure, his jaw clenching a few times before he said, "I didn't invite you in here to trade insults."

"You didn't? Darn."

"Sit down," he said, tossing his mail on his desk. One of the envelopes skidded across the surface and landed at her feet.

"Thank you, but I prefer to stand."

"Suit yourself." He took his seat like a king settling into a throne, then used the silent ploy again. CJ didn't let it bother her. After nearly a minute of staring at each other in a battle of wills he finally said, "You've done it this time, haven't you, Celia?"

"It's Mizz Celia to you, Miles. And what exactly have I done?"

"You know damn well what," he scoffed, "or do I have to recite the conversation I had with Mr. Hamilton?"

George Hamilton, owner of *DRIVE Magazine*, and a bigger jerk than Miles. Well, not exactly. Nobody could be a bigger jerk than Miles.

"Are you perhaps referring to my first appearance on national television?"

He smiled. "Yes, I am, though I confess I had my doubts about George's speculation that you and Danvers were, ahh, *lovers*." Once again, he eyed her up and down.

CJ gave him her own brittle smile. "If by that little dig you're referring to the fact that I'm not his type, then you're right, I'm not. But then again, he's not my type either. Slimy little worms are the type of men that find me interesting, as you well know."

His face hardened.

"Or have you forgotten about the supply closet?" She smiled sweetly.

His eyes narrowed. "Celia, making me angry isn't going to help your cause."

She pasted a look of contrition on her face. "Am I making you angry? Gee, Miles, I'm sorry. And here I was trying to be nice to you after all the asinine, idiotic, down-and-dirty things you've done to me lately."

"I never did anything to you, Celia."

"Oh bull, Miles. You've done nothing but make my life hell out of a petty sense of revenge. And to top it all off, you just sent me on an assignment I had no business going on."

His expression turned into a glare. "I sent you on a job most reporters would have killed to go on—"

"*Field* reporters, Miles. Most *experienced* field reporters would have killed to go on. I've only been with DRIVE for a few months. You should have sent someone who actually knew something about off-road racing."

"Well, I sent you," he snapped, going around to stand in front of his chair. "But I should have known you weren't capable of doing the job."

"But I did complete the assignment, you little shit."

"Only because you slept with Bryce Danvers."

She took a step toward his desk, leaning close to him as she could stand. "It might surprise you to know this, Miles. Some men care more for what's on the inside, than the outside."

"Well, if he had sex with you, that's patently obvious. But we don't pay people to screw while on the job."

"No, they just pay assholes like you to make passes at any and all female employees." There was a time to swear, and then there was *a time to swear.*

"All right." He banged his fist on his desk. "I've had enough of your insults. I was going to see if we could work this out. Put you on probation or something, but it's apparent you could care less about this job."

"Oh, bull, Miles," she scoffed. "The only reason you'd go on letting me work here is to suit your own masochistic needs."

"That's not true."

"Yes it is, and you know it. You need help, Miles. Go get yourself some counseling."

"That does it. Get out. You're fired." He pointed to the door like a blustering, irate cartoon character; steam billowed out of his ears in great clouds, and his face turned fire engine red.

"My pleasure. And you can't fire me. I quit. And the minute I'm out the door, I'm seeing a lawyer about a sexual harassment suit." She turned away, opened the door.

"Good luck with that," he called out. "Especially after how you handled your last assignment."

"Handled being the operative word," she said with a cocky smile even though inside she was starting to panic.

This was it. She was finally leaving *DRIVE.*

"Your key, Celia."

She swung her chin up. "You want my office key? Really, Miles. Are you afraid I might break back in and paint spineless prick on your door?"

"Not even you would be so stupid." He sat down abruptly.

THHHHHPUUUUUUUUT.

"What the—" Miles shot back up, turning back to the chair and picking up a red-plastic bladder.

"Did you do this?" he asked, holding out the Whoopee

Cushion, his expression enraged.

No. No, she hadn't. But she wished she knew who had, she'd kiss the person. And then she caught the brand name. Toyco. That was Bryce's compan—

Slowly, she turned toward the door.

And there he was, staring at her with his blue, blue eyes and looking like an L.L. Bean model in his khaki pants and off white polo. "Hi, honey."

His voice washed over her; familiar and oh so achingly sweet.

Oh, God.

It was too late. She'd already fallen.

"Well, if it isn't Mr. Heartthrob himself," Miles said sarcastically.

She continued to stare at Bryce, study him, absorb him. He looked tired.

He also looked a bit perturbed with her, or maybe with Miles. She had her answer when he said, "And you must be Miles Van *Dick*, the man who glues condoms to his penis."

Her ex-boss's face turned a florid, angry color. Slowly, he pushed himself to his feet; his brown eyes latched on to her. "You told him about that?"

Suddenly, she wanted to laugh, maybe it was nerves, or maybe it was happiness. She was suddenly giddy. "Of course I did."

Miles blinked at her. "You little—"

"Ahh, ahh, ahh, Miles," she interrupted. "It's not nice to call ex-employees names." She fluttered her eyelashes at him.

His face grew even more thunderous. "Get out," he hissed. His eyes latched onto Bryce. "You, too."

"What? You mean you don't want us to stay? And I was enjoying our chat sooo much," CJ prodded.

He looked back at her. "Get out," he repeated. "Neither of you have any business being here." His lip curled. "Especially you, CJ, not anymore."

"Believe me, Miles, I'm more grateful about that than you could possibly know."

She turned to Bryce, but Bryce wasn't looking at her, he was staring at Miles and it was safe to say he was infuriated.

"You're the one who has no business being here."

CJ felt her heart swell. He was defending her. Wow.

"Oh, yeah?" Miles clipped out.

"Yeah."

"Is that a threat?"

"Take it however you want. And it may interest you to know, I *made love* to CJ because to me she's the most beautiful woman I've ever met."

CJ's breath caught, that might be laying it on a bit thick, but when he turned to look at her and she saw the tenderness in his eyes...

And her breath caught.

"C'mon, CJ. Let's get out of here." He held out his hand and she took it.

That was when it hit her. She wasn't afraid of falling in love with him anymore. Truth was, she'd fallen for him the moment she'd spotted him standing in Miles's door.

"You're through in journalism," Miles called after her. "I'll see to it that you never—"

The rest of his words were cut off as Bryce ducked behind her and slammed the door. His gaze met hers, "I learned that one from you."

She wanted to laugh. She wanted to cry. She wanted to kiss him to death. God, it was so good to see him. She understood in that instant how much she'd missed him. Grabbing his hand, she headed for her office.

The steady hum of keyboards clicking dwindled to nothingness. CJ could practically feel the eyes boring a hole in the back of her rayon jacket. She held her head high and all but dragged Bryce away. She needed to get her purse, then they could talk somewhere private.

Bryce didn't give her the opportunity. The minute they stepped inside, he closed the door. CJ spun back to face him. And suddenly, she didn't know what to say. She wanted to throw herself into his arms, wanted to apologize for being such a coward, instead she firmly clasped her hands behind her back and rocked back on her heels. "It's good to see you."

He stared down at her, his blue eyes unwavering. "You left me." It wasn't an accusation, merely a pronouncement. His husky, southern drawl washed over her like a caress.

She felt as low as foot fungus. "I noticed."

He continued to stare, and the look in his eyes was changing, growing softer. "You didn't even leave me your phone number."

She looked away, blinking back sudden tears, but her eyes were drawn back to his in the next instant. "I know."

He took a step toward her. "I tried everything to get it."

She lifted a brow. "You did?" And as the ramification of what he'd said sank in, happiness blossomed inside her. The inside of her stomach fluttered like a butterfly. More dratted tears hovered.

He took another step. She clenched her hands at her sides.

"I, ahh, I thought for sure Harry would have it."

"He didn't."

She swallowed again, suddenly realizing she was about to start blubbering like an idiot. "Oh."

He took another step. "I finally called the owner of this magazine to get it."

Her vision was blurring. Damn it, she would not cry. "Oh, Bryce."

"He said the only way he'd give me your number was if I bought the magazine." He met her gaze again, all the love in the world captured in his eyes. "So I did."

"Did what?" she asked, feeling like she'd left her brain back in Miles's office.

"Bought *DRIVE Magazine.*"

She stared at him incredulously. "You didn't?"

"Yes, I did."

"Just for my phone number?"

"You're worth it, CJ."

Her heart hammered in her chest at the look in his eyes.

"I love you."

She loved him too. It seemed impossible, she had no idea how it had happened over the course of a few days, but she did.

"I don't want to spend another day away from you," he added.

She couldn't stand it anymore. He opened his arms, she sank into them, her hands shaking, the world doing back flips. He smelled like pine. Beautiful, foresty pine.

"I love you so much." His voice was hoarse with emotion. "I know it sounds incredible after we've known each other so short a time, but I feel the rightness of this in the marrow of my bones."

"I know," she murmured, pressing her cheek against his chest. "I feel the same way too."

"Then why'd you leave me?" he asked, rocking her, holding her, hugging her.

"Because I was scared to death."

He drew back, framing her face with his hands and swiping at her tears with his thumbs. "You little idiot."

She swallowed back more tears. "I know."

And then he bent down to kiss her and CJ felt her legs give out from under her, but it didn't matter. Bryce held on like he'd never let her go, but that was fine with CJ, because she'd never let him let her go, either. He deepened the kiss and when his taste flooded into her mouth, she realized something...

They belonged together.

Bryce must have thought so too, because she heard him whisper her name, and then she heard no more. She was lost in the taste of him, in the touch of him, in the smell of him. Nothing penetrated except the persistent sound of music. The sound swelled and grew until finally she drew back and said, "What the heck is that?"

"What?" he murmured against her lips.

"The music." She pulled away, turning to look out the window behind her desk.

Bryce's kiss rattled her brain so much, that at first she didn't believe what she was seeing. But when the images of a marching band in all its shiny splendor didn't fade, she realized it wasn't a hallucination at all.

The band stood in the middle of the parking lot, white and red uniforms glaring in the sun. A fuzzy-hatted conductor waved his baton up and down like a crazed artist painting on an invisible canvas. Through the window came the faint sound of "You Light up My Life".

She turned back to Bryce suspiciously. "What is this?"

"What is what?" Bryce asked innocently.

But he couldn't fool her. She gestured toward the window with her hand. "*That,*" she motioned. And then she saw a sheet of paper flutter down from the sky. It landed on a small bush just outside her window. Soon there was another, followed by another and another. "What the—"

They were drifting down like giant, white snowflakes. Hundreds of them, thousands of them, one even drifted in front of her face, but this one was held in Bryce's hand.

CJ Randall, will you marry me? it said

She gasped, covering her mouth with her hands. Slowly, she turned back to Bryce, barely able to see him through the sheen of tears clouding her eyes.

"Will you?" he asked softly, dropping the paper on the floor.

She blinked up at him, unable to think, unable to breathe, unable, even, to nod her head. And then all of sudden the tears she'd been holding back broke like a dam whose floodgates had opened. She bawled, just bawled her damn eyes out. Jeesh, it was humiliating.

"Ah, CJ, honey," Bryce said softly. "Is that a yes?"

She nodded.

He opened his arms, smiling at her, a smile like she'd never seen before. Gone was Bryce the flirt. In his place stood Bryce the lover, Bryce the friend; Bryce the soon-to-be husband.

She loved them all.

He might be Trouble, but he was her Trouble. She flung herself into his arms, closing her eyes against the tears that refused to shut off. It was several minutes later that CJ murmured against Bryce's very wet chest, "Bryce?"

"What, honey?" he asked tenderly.

She pulled back, smiling up at him impishly, and wiping at her tears. "Can we go fire Miles now? Because I know this perfect person to hire as editor—"

Epilogue

"There's a huge crowd on hand today to watch the last leg of the Baja 1000," the sportscaster's voice blared through the television set, the camera panning over the crowd.

"That's right, Dave, and it's a beautiful day here in the California desert. Weather forecast is sunny and eighty degrees. A perfect day for the finish of this prestigious event. And the big story here is the Toyco team."

"I couldn't agree with you more, Ralph. Five starts, three wins, two seconds…an impressive record."

"What's even more impressive is the driver."

"You've got that right, Ralph. A whole lot of sponsors would give a year's income to latch onto a driver like that."

"Word is there've even *been* an offer or two to steal the driver away."

"Yeah, but all of off road racing knows the Toyco team is a family affair. I hear they even bring their four-year-old son to the races."

"Well it looks like he'll be able to join his parents in the winners' circle today because the trucks have just emerged from the desert foothills, and it looks like the Toyco team's still in the lead."

The camera zoomed in for a close-up, showing two trucks

racing through the desert, dust clouds pluming in their wakes.

"That's right, Ralph. And right behind the Danvers' vehicle is the Toyco truck driven by Nick Seavers. And behind him is the Star Oil truck driven by Harry Santini."

"And there's another story. One would think that the Danvers' would go easy on the man who introduced them to racing, but the two teams are always running neck and neck. Rumor has it they're even fielding a new type of race car, one of the X-treme Racing cars."

"*That* ought to be an interesting series," Dave said. "It's being billed as a no-holds-barred, anything goes type of series."

"Kind of like off road racing, huh, Dave?"

"You got that right."

The camera followed the trucks as they drew closer to the spectators.

"And here they come, Dave. Boy are they hauling."

"But it looks like, yup, it's going to be the Toyco team in Victory Circle for the fourth time this year."

"What a great finish. Now, let's go down to Stan, who's standing by at the winners' circle."

The camera switched to a man holding a microphone. In the background the Toyco race truck drew to a halt. The man turned toward the vehicle, microphone held out as he waited for the driver to emerge. A moment later a figure slipped out of the window, the Toyco logo emblazoned across his firesuit, only it wasn't a him, as the camera revealed an instant later. It was at her, a her who revealed shoulder length brown hair when she removed her helmet.

"Mrs. Danvers, you've had an incredible season."

"Thanks, Stan," CJ said with a huge smile.

"But I gotta ask you a question our viewers are dying to

know. Is there any truth to the rumors you might drive in another racing league?"

CJ turned toward her husband, laughing. "Oh, I don't know, Stan. Maybe."

"The garage is abuzz about the X-treme Racing League."

"Really? I wonder why?"

Stan could tell he was being stonewalled. With a good-natured smile, he glanced at Bryce and changed the subject. "We hear Mr. Danvers is a difficult man to work for, is that true?"

CJ smiled. *This* question she could answer. After five years of marriage, Bryce's answering grin was filled with as much love as it had been the day she'd married him. It was also just as wicked. "Oh, he's Trouble, all right," she teased. "My kind of Trouble."

Author's Note

I hope you enjoyed Playboy Prankster. In it, I get to combine two things I love. Humor and racing. And speaking of racing, this book would not be in existence today without the invaluable assistance of Steve Cartwright. Steve told me about S.C.O.R.E., chits, and other things off-road racing. As such, the errors in this book are due to the author's blonde hair, not Steve...much as I'd like to blame a man for my mistakes.

Smiles and giggles,
Pamela

About the Author

With over a million books in print, Pamela Britton likes to call herself the best known author nobody's ever heard of. Of course, that's begun to change thanks to a certain licensing agreement with that little racing organization known as NASCAR.

But before the glitz and glamour of NASCAR, Pamela wrote books that were frequently voted the best of the best by *The Detroit Free Press*, Barnes & Noble (two years in a row) and RT BOOKclub Magazine. She's won numerous writing awards, including the National Reader's Choice Award, and a nomination for Romance Writers of America's Golden Heart.

When not writing romance novels, Pamela competes all over kingdom come on her American Quarter Horse, Bippidy Boppin Along, aka: Bippy, the Bipster or Bubba-Dubba. Check her schedule. She might be coming to a town near you.

Pamela loves to hear from readers. Feel free to contact her through her web site at www.pamelabritton.com or through Facebook at www.facebook.com/pamelabritton.

Some rules just beg to be broken.

Just Like That
© 2010 Erin Nicholas
The Bradfords, Book 2

Danika Steffen can take care of herself. Watching her mother slowly succumb to muscular dystrophy convinced Danika that total independence is the only way to go. Anything that needs fixing, she's got the tools. So what if she's never had an orgasm. No one really needs one, right?

Sam Bradford is good at two things: his job as a paramedic, and seducing women. Being dependable? Not so much. Losing his father at age fifteen tore a permanent hole in his life, and now he's determined never to let anyone need him that much. Enjoying women, though, is definitely on the menu. As long as they understand his unbreakable rule: one night only. Until a date with Danika Steffen ends not in her bed, but with a trip to the ER.

Danika may have a broken wrist, but Sam's the one suffering…an intense case of guilt. And instead of doing things to her, he only wants to do things for her. Which would drive her crazy if not for the sneaking suspicion that Sam needs a little TLC too. And damned if she doesn't want to be the one to give it…

Warning: Contains an I'll-do-it-myself girl who can fix anything, a commitment-phobic guy who can't fix anything, and a whole new way to look at butter. Yes, butter.

Available now in ebook and print from Samhain Publishing.

GREAT CHEAP FUN

Discover eBooks!

THE FASTEST WAY TO GET THE HOTTEST NAMES

Get your favorite authors on your favorite reader, long before they're out in print! Ebooks from Samhain go wherever you go, and work with whatever you carry—Palm, PDF, Mobi, Kindle, nook, and more.

WWW.SAMHAINPUBLISHING.COM